ONE LAST WALTZ

ONE LAST WALTZ

by
Ethan Mordden

St. Martin's Press
New York

To my family

Library of Congress Cataloging-in-Publication Data

Mordden, Ethan.
  One last waltz.

  I. Title.
PS3563.07717054 1986   813'.54   86–3665
ISBN 0–312–58528–4

First Edition
10 9 8 7 6 5 4 3 2 1

IF THE READER
WOULD BE SO KIND

The forerunner of the novel was the saga, an episodic tale spun out of an oral tradition, frequently on the life and death of a hero, the swelling of a great war, or the fortunes of a family: *Beowulf*, *Igor's Campaign*, *Gunnlaugr Serpent's-Tooth*. Such tales, for all their length, come without many of the naturalistic details that we take for granted in the novel—the painting in of environmental, conversational, and psychological conditions, or that sort of Dickensian *kto kowo* that can take twenty pages simply to explain how a minor character arrived at a certain point in the pages of a narrative.

Some sagas, however, may claim the peculiar convention of Dickens' day, the intrusive narrator, often a Christian scribe—or several scribes working at different times—taking down a folk tale with extracurricular emendations, resulting, frequently, in an arresting confusion of tones not unlike the layered multiplicity of an archeological dig. I have put myself into such a narrator's shoes, though—Christians be warned—I serve a personal, and eccentric, church.

This, then, is a tale with conversations, a novel without many explanations, on the fortunes of a family. It might be an old story from the middle ages, pulled into modern times, its witches and demon coincidences intact but dressed to pass. There is no great war, no clear hero. One event leads to another without elaboration. It has one beginning and one end but three middles, whose combined purpose is to show how a given domestic atmosphere can produce three quite different children—and, as well, how different that atmosphere can feel to each child: depending on what you got and what you wanted.

CONTENTS

The author wishes to acknowledge art director Andy Carpenter's ingenious suggestion for the cover design, which brings home (literally) the book's central image, and Izume Inoue's reverberant execution. One almost hears the Victrola's sorry music.

In particular, I must hail the crucial guidance of my editor, Michael Denneny, who is as sharp a storyteller as any of us; and of my agent, Dorothy Pittman, who never tires of asking the musical question, "How old are they supposed to be in this scene?" Dorothy, We kiss in a shadow. Michael, Carefully taught.

PROLOGUE

Each family bears three secrets, secrets so damning that we would give up friendship, love, money, perhaps even our lives to preserve them. One secret conceals something wanted, one secret something known, and one secret something done. What we want we must not have. What we know made us vulnerable. What we did is unforgivable. Yet some in the world do get the secret thing they want: these are the criminals. Some pretend that what they know does not exist: these are the living wounded. And some are forgiven: these are the rest of us.

Nora Keogh took her secrets with her into the coffin, for she had died suddenly, thrown down a stairwell, the whole five floors. She did not utter a sound when she was murdered, and no witnesses came forth. Nor did anyone know of a reason someone would have for the killing of Nora Keogh. And such is the strain of life, especially among the Irish, that everyone and his father had no trouble taking Nora Keogh's death for suicide. There were notions here and about. There was talk. But you'd have to be the Pope to die without there being talk of some sort, would you not? Even then there'd be notions. The Irish live on notions, for there have been times when they had scarcely anything else to live on at all.

Dublin Johnny Keogh, Nora's husband that was, determined that her wake should be remembered in legend as a last hurrah for the old ways. We're often hearing that our seniors were our betters, that they carried themselves with a vitality and color we cannot feel or see today, that tradition is being watered down, like the last bottle of whiskey in a party that defied exhaustion and lived till Sunday morning. No one knows how to make a party as the Irish know the art, yet the wake, their most essential party— the one at which the most intent truths are told—is becoming as dreary and formal as a tea.

How long has it been since you drank to the peace of the departed with the open coffin right there before you? How long since you heard the groans of the survivors, a true keening, or saw the sons sorrowing over the body as if they would give their lives to bring it back to life? For who can weep a woman lost as her boys can, if they have the stuff in them? Some say that parents bear the load of grief for children, the mothers especially, who brought them forth in misery; but I say it's children who most persuasively long for a dead parent, the boys for their mas, especially. With their das it's somehow a more variable thing, for a boy can mislike a disquieting da, even hate a bad one. And some are bad. But even a bitter and treacherous ma will excite a boy's need for love—and, let it be said, straight out, that Nora Keogh was not thought peerless in the neighborhood. Years before, she had been, maybe, a character of some pleasant renown, if not a loving woman then a romantic one. There was a day when she felt her Johnny as tree leaves feel the wind. Yet did she raise her boys right? Did she set a fine table, cherish her people, earn the devotion of friends? You could not say so. Nor was she a one to spare a Saturday sinner a Sunday accusation, or to soothe a quarrel with the wisdom of the uninvolved. She was, in fact, the sort of woman who can get herself killed, so no wonder there were notions. The Father himself was hard put to recite upon her qualities, and in the end had to beg assistance from some of his more imaginative parishioners. And did they not help him solely out of respect for the cloth, and for the good of the wake?

And the poor children, think of them: three boys alone with just the father to look after them, and he a harder wall than even she was, if such be possible. They say every Irish town has one hard one somewhere, no matter what the weather or how the potato crop is doing, and, in the Irish town called New York, it was a toss-up as to who was the harder, Dublin Johnny or his Nora. You should have seen, when it was the boys' turn to file past their ma in her coffin, how Dublin Johnny dug his great grasping hands into their shoulder bones, as if detaining them against their will, or making them be quiet, or just putting on a show of forcing them somehow, even if for no purpose, just to force them. And we others are asking, Can you pass the hardness on through the blood?

The boys were the last to view Nora. All others with the right had gone before, few—it was noted—in anything like sorrow. Some were curious, to see the dead so, for a true wake was a rare thing in 1968. Some were polite only, and passed before the earthly body of Nora Keogh with their eyes closed like Protestants, thinking that somewhere in the very idea of a wake was a blasphemy. Many were far enough advanced in the splendor of their cups to offer stimulating farewells—and they the sort who wouldn't know what to say to a bus driver. Nora's three boys were silent, but Dublin Johnny was never a man to lose a word. Stopping the musicians, he announced, "And now for the boys' last prayers, and their solemn moment of fare-thee-well, for which a little silence from you all."

And so he grabbed the oldest, John the younger, then twenty, and tall and broad like his father, with his father's bright eye and deep jaw, and his devil's smile that all the women loved at first sight, though young Johnny smiled but seldom; and Dublin Johnny held his oldest son at the coffin to gaze upon dead Nora, and the boy showed nothing in his face, except that at the last moment, when a few of those standing by saw his shoulders shake as he knelt to cross himself. But by then all present were thoroughly weakened by drink and nostalgia and the effort of raising up a lamentation for politeness' sake, so who could be certain what he might have seen or not seen?

Then came the middle boy, Parnell Michael, seventeen, and his mother's favorite, and he was weeping. "She loved you, man," cried Dublin Johnny, some say with a bitter edge in his voice, "and you must treasure her memory so." Young Parnell looked on Nora a long moment, and he crossed himself with a most fitting poignance when he knelt.

"Now this one," says Dublin Johnny, and pulls up Dennis, fifteen years old and half an orphan. And, again, there were those with an eye for a telling picture who swear they saw the boy glaring in a derogatory manner at his da. Then Dublin Johnny, suddenly struck by an idea, grabs Dennis by the head and looks true and long at him, and he sees in that moment that Dennis knows who threw Nora down the stairwell of a brownstone on East Fifty-fourth Street.

But Dublin Johnny pushes young Dennis away, without waiting for him to kneel and make a last cross for the late Nora Keogh.

"Now," Dublin Johnny thunders, "let's get the devil into this party, so we'll have something to repent of next confession!"

And he slams the lid of the coffin shut.

PART ONE

The King of Tara Founds His Kingdom

There was the matter of a small inheritance, and recalcitrant cousins, and a lawyer, curse the race of them. Even in good times, no Irishman can afford to turn his back on a bit of money found, as it were, in the law; though when, I ask you, has Ireland seen good times in any season since the landlords came? It was 1936, and Cullin Keogh of the town of Bri Leith was so poor he was facing the prospect of temperance, what with credit at Murry's pub long gone and no work of any usual sort on offer. His wife holds what money there is. To his longing look, as his friends Galloping Toomey and Frank Dray pass on the road on their way to Murry's of an evening, she tells him, "Drink rain. It's free."

Just then, dearly in time, comes the news from the city: an uncle by the same name, Cullin Keogh, dies in Dublin.

"He will have died happy in such a place," says Cullin, "where there's a pub on every corner and a pack of friends instead of two, and everlasting credit. A man can manage in Dublin."

This uncle has left a certain sum of money to be divided among his relatives, and Cullin is thinking he might set off for Dublin and

3

take his share home with him before the lawyer legalizes it away in fees.

"I'll make a settlement on him," says Cullin, more confidently the more he tells it. "I'll take it off him if I have to. I'll show him law, this Dublin barrister and practitioner!" Cullin knows the words, which is the second reason why he, a poor man, has prestige in Bri Leith. Now there's letters he'll open and show, two letters from the lawyer—and one could not say which is the more confusing for all the Brits in Derry—and one letter from a cousin and her husband that seems unfriendly, even censorious. "What do you make of that, now?" Cullin asks you, to show you what an important citizen he is, to receive letters from Dublin.

Finally his wife says, "Then you'd best go to Dublin, and make your settlement, and cease your talking of it at long last."

Cullin is quiet at this.

"I've silver for it, come to that," she says. "And you will take Johnny with you, to assure an agreeable visit with the solicitor."

And Cullin brightens at that.

For his son Johnny, the first reason why Cullin has prestige in Bri Leith, is, at seventeen, the biggest male in the locale. Then you must consider that Johnny is fleet, especially when chasing down a neighbor, many yards distant, who may have made a questionable remark. Johnny is a figure of some intelligent authority even at his young age, not least because, on a certain night not long before this, the publican Murry offers, for the third time and not so politely now, to collect the glasses, and clear the taps, and close his shop for the night, and Johnny speaks up to say, "You'll crawl home if you do, sir," and extends his right fist the way he always did, twice, rapidly, knuckles down, then turning them up in your face, as if showing his lack of weapons, to take you by the flesh and bone of the matter. So you may imagine that they are few in Bri Leith or anywhere else who will damn Johnny's father Cullin Keogh for a whining, stingy bastard.

To his face.

Johnny props up Cullin's reputation and menaces those of the girls. One day his sweetheart Jetty Hoolan says to him, "Turn off

4

your eyes, Johnny Keogh. Or buy shutters for them. It's not fit to see, what they're showing."

And Johnny replies, running it slowly over his tongue, "When can I, lady?" Like that, straight out, for this man is all appetite and nothing else. When he hungers, he believes in food. When he thirsts, he believes in whiskey. When he worries, he believes in God.

Jetty can make no reply, and runs off, glad it's daylight still and he cannot chase her far without the witness of Jetty's older sister, Mary. "That's a bad, honest man," Jetty thinks of Johnny, with the great wood of her door between them. "That's a man will shake you by the neck if you don't give him what he wants."

She wants Johnny, though she fears him as much as she likes him. That is a form of love for some. And, truth to tell, she misses him the three days he's in Dublin with his father making their claim on the will.

"I've no money for it," Cullin moans. "Where'll I be staying?" he cries. "The lawyer and his tricks," he mopes. Stringy, sullen stock, the Keoghs. Who knows where such as Johnny came from?

"From God's laugh," says his mother to this question, when someone asks. She is as sudden as her son, ready to shock. When Johnny extends his fists to her, she slaps his face, and he grabs her hand and holds it to his cheek and sighs.

"The dread faker," she calls him; but she's in his spell the same as any, and gives him one silver crown for the trip just before they leave and tells him, "Mind you buy something treasurable with it. Something true."

"Nothing's true but me," he answers, with a grin, and his jaw. And up she is, to slap him, for all the good it's worth. She has particular rights, no doubt, as the only woman in Bri Leith who doesn't think about having Johnny Keogh.

The Johnny Keoghs of the world were made for Dublin, for a city place, and they know it from the moment they walk in. They see the scope of things, the expansiveness of the social contract, the room there must be for arrangements of various kinds. A town like

Bri Leith is a lovely place for knowing all about everyone and being certain of the things about you, but it is not long before a man realizes that all you can know about people is whether they like you or fear you, and that the things about you are nothing but birth, toil, and death.

A city, however, holds an inexhaustible variety of people and things, and Dublin, the dull beast of brown and gray, is a great city. If Paris is arrogant and London is facetious, Dublin is Irish, so even the least sophisticated son of the race may make himself welcome there with little trouble, though all about him are strangers.

If the citizens of Bri Leith made trips to Dublin, they would have arranged to stay with relatives; but none in Bri Leith ever went anywhere, except to Koine or Fenny, the two towns on either side of it; and which was the less notable of the two, one would be hard put to say. Koine was wet and Fenny was old; or Fenny had six dens of public amusement and Koine had three widows under the age of thirty. Dublin was wet and old and boasted an endless supply of pubs and widows. One got there the same way one got to Koine or Fenny—by walking and cadging rides—but it took longer. Cullin, at the halfway point of his life and in any case never a hearty man, arrived in Dublin beyond the prospect of anything but bed, though it was scarcely dark in a young summer and the city was shining from lamp to lamp, in the drinking rooms and the faces. Johnny, impressed by his own awe, missed the nuances of fear and regret that passed across his father's face.

"I'll see you to quarters, da," said Johnny, gazing about him.

"But where?" Cullin worried. "Where in the kingdom of Tara, I'm asking?"

Experienced travelers—which these, of course, were not—will tell you that in Dublin you needn't ask anyone for information: he'll give it to you anyway. Still, Johnny stopped a passerby— tweed coat, curious eyes, unlit pipe—to learn where he and his da might put up.

"That would depend," says the Dubliner, "on whether you're solvent or no." Lighting his pipe.

6

"We're solvent," said Johnny, quietly, his temper on call. "What do you take us for?"

"Strangers," says he. Then waits.

Johnny, interested in learning whether or not he's being made a fool of, and eager, if he is, to make remedy, waits, too.

"Ah," says the Dubliner. "A listener."

"If you'd play the good soul for us now," pleaded Cullin. "If you would. For I've a sense of misadventure upon me such as would still the Cuchullain himself."

"Then," says the Dubliner, "it's Mistress Firing's you'd be wanting, in Montgomery Street. A very poetic accommodation, there." It was, by hap, just a few streets up the high. He would take them to it. Better, he would vouch for them personally to Mistress Firing—who, being a woman vocationally subject to the comings and goings of men she hardly knew by real name or county, did surely prefer to have her guests accounted for by some familiarity, so to speak. Indeed, she was known to be sometimes contentious with strangers.

"Ah, that is kind of you," said Cullin. "But quickly now, for if I don't put my feet down the long way soon enough, I'll have to bury them, for sure they'll die on me."

"How far have you come?" asked the Dubliner as they walked up the boulevard, the question meaning, What's your region and your reason for coming among us? The most Irish of questions.

Johnny let Cullin hold Bri Leith's end of the conversation in place, the better to concentrate on his surroundings. Although the most acknowledged male in Bri Leith—and that for a host of reasons—Johnny had expected, if dimly and without apprehension, to be overwhelmed in this great town. But, scarce entered, he seemed to feel lightheaded, even inspired. His da, who knew nothing of anything, said "A man can manage in Dublin." In this, Johnny sensed, Cullin might for once be right. A city supplies to each man's need: you simply walk in and ask. Walk into Dublin and ask for Mistress Firing's, why not?

"Ardrey Quinn," Mistress Firing growls at the door, seeing Quinn and meaning no respect.

"Here are guests," he replies.

"So," says she. "So." Something less than a welcome.

"Ah, you've the air of the Banshee of Dingle, when she returned from the midnight dancing at Glasharrin to find her daughters all married to sailors."

"Quinn," she notes, "you're a bad word for scoundrel." She eyes the Keoghs. "Friends of the Quinn?" she asks.

"Let a traveller come to Dublin on the Liffey, says I," says Quinn, "and who but Mistress Firing to see to them? The fey contessa of Montgomery Street!"

"Now you're a bad word for bastard, Quinn."

"She's a rogue," Quinn confided to his guests.

"My da wants to sleep," Johnny puts in. "We'll be grateful for a cheap room."

"Oh you will?" says Mistress Firing. "With your fine, strong voice. You'll be grateful."

"The boy'll want a look around Dublin first, no doubt," suggests Quinn. "Now he's here."

"I'd not be one to philosophize in my doorway," Mistress Firing notes, taking in the measure of Johnny Keogh with a bold look for a woman. "But here's a fast piece of Irish sod and a slow week come together. There must be something in it, Quinn."

"There's Ireland growing in it," twitters Quinn, "and the crop is love."

Mistress Firing backs up to let the strangers into her house. "The crop of Ireland," utters she, "is famine."

"Show me a man's people," says Ardrey Quinn in the pub called The Voyager, "and I'll know him."

"My people," Johnny answers, "are the men of Tara, the true kingdom of Ireland, as it was in the great bygone ages and must be forever along."

"I'm with you, lad. But a man's truest kingdom is his family. We are each a king, then, and sure of our cohort."

"The man who is sure of anyone is a leaking fool."

8

"You're the young one to speak a cynic's part," Quinn notes thoughtfully.

"I'm big, to speak how I please," Johnny says, a bit loudly. Men turned to look.

"You may be sure of children," says Quinn, signalling for the refilling of the glasses. "There is nothing as keen as the little girl's trust in her father, or the little boy's admiration. Sure, have you seen them gathered to sing a wee song in honor of their father on his natal day?"

"I'm telling you," Johnny insists, "it's no one you can count on. Each player has his intentions, do you see?"

"Do I, now? Did not the Wicked Fairy of Follanerry wish her entire court bound into stone to still their gabbling tongues, as were rippling with tales of the Fairy's facetious contract with the Lord of Darnell?"

"Did she? That's fast of her. Sharp. You must move quickly, or how often does the chance bite?"

"More often in a place like Dublin," Quinn ventured, "than in your little village of home, where everyone's a farmer and each day's cousin to the last day and the next."

"What's in Dublin, then?"

"All the kinds, lad. That's what I'm telling you. That's Dublin. Each day a fresh one, with as many strangers in it as cousins. And what's that but liberty, lad? The only liberty an Irishman ever sees, it may well be. Consider now, who owns Ireland?"

"The English," said a man behind Quinn, quietly listening till this.

"And that right enough," Quinn replied. "Now, who is it owns the Irish people?"

"The Pope," said another man, looming up from one of the tables. "First of the absentee landlords."

"Thus," Quinn comes back. "And who owns Dublin?"
Silence.

"No one," said Quinn in the hush. "Dublin is free."

Johnny Keogh was not a one to listen, for in Bri Leith there was

9

little worth hearing. Now, in The Voyager, he gulped hock and kept his ears open. For it had befallen him to wonder if he ought to dwell forever in Bri Leith, or undertake some less innocent existence in a more elated location.

"Is Dublin an honorable place?" one of the newcomers wondered.

"Or beautiful?" added the other.

"Ah," said Quinn, eager to enlarge. "Are honor and beauty the themes of a great city? Tell me the themes of a place and I'll know it." He turned to Johnny. "A man's people, and the themes of his whereabouts—that is his history. Now, if his people be loving and fair in their judgment, and their themes be notable, I will admire their story. Then what if his people be needlessly fierce, and his themes a wanton, curse-of-God bitterness and envy? Why then, Dublin will give him no joy. Even Dublin."

So the night ran, in talk and thinking, and in shifting tides of listening ears to riddle Quinn, and in Johnny's standing his share of the rounds, an almost combative gesture for a village lad, till at last all melted away into the night to the tapster's surly pleas, Quinn guiding sodden Johnny Keogh back to Mistress Firing's.

"Gets the boy as useless as a Druid in the confessional," said the lady of the house when they arrived. "That's Quinn."

"A fine, entertaining type of chap," said Johnny. "A high bard at my court of Tara."

"A high meddling booby at any pub in Dublin, you mean," says Mistress Firing.

"Yet I've dainty tricks to inspire a man's morals," Quinn returns. "Sure, we'd best give the lad a cup of tea before he sleeps, so he'll wake up all restored, so to say."

"Restore him?" says Mistress Firing, not kindly; but she leads the way to her drab kitchen. The pot, cup, and spoons. Quinn stirs idly here. Johnny, half asleep, sits at the table.

"Mistress Firing," says Quinn, "provides. Her blunt way is but a mask, to spare Dublin the savage warmth of her compassion. Mistress Firing is generous."

"Let the boy take his tea and hush, Quinn!"

Johnny smiled at Mistress Firing.

"Now, that's a smile," says she, "that has the girls all sporty as widows in May, I'm certain."

"A young man in Dublin," observes Quinn, lighting his pipe, "has great events."

"It's strong tea," says Mistress Firing, "but comforting."

"She brews an earnest cup," says Quinn, puffing.

And they watch him drink.

"Smile again, will you, now," Mistress Firing urges. "I like a country smile in my kitchen now and again."

Johnny puts down his cup and smiles.

"Oh," says she, "a lovely thing, that is."

Stumbling to his bed after the long, inspiriting day, Johnny scarce noticed it odd that he was not in the same room as his da, and he fell into such heavy slumber that he did not awaken when she crept into his bed and wrapped her limbs about his body and kissed his neck. Then she was running her hands about him and freeing him of his things, and he blundered awake.

"Who is it?" he said.

"Hush," she whispered. "Touch and know." He put his hands on her, felt the smooth skin and firm breasts of a young woman, so tight and trim. She shuddered as his hands moved faster and wider, in frantic question, his grogginess spinning away. He kissed her, wondering what sort of trouble would come of it, for in his world everything wondrous was forbidden.

He became rough, the Church-scarred, furtive bumpkin, and she held him back. "Be sweet," she whispered, and he was, then, learning to savor the pleasure of the slow rhythm, going slower, his mouth playing with her mouth. He touched her nipples, almost crying out in joy, and he stroked her thighs. Then he did groan; but she was silent. She put her arms about him again, and held him so close he could breathe with her, and the tiniest motion of her body, touching all of his, made him dizzy.

He felt of her, and was so warm he made as if to have her just then, but she was before him, sage, and whispered, "Wait," and taught him the lore of tongue and fingertips. She made him lie back and bear her touch without himself moving till he would nearly scream, and so still she was when he touched her that he must bury his face in her breast to hear her breath.

Then he was wild and must have her, and she knew by his noise and grasping that he would not be held back. She whispered, "Yes —but first kiss my eyes."

And he did so, trying to be gentle in spite of his eagerness. He grazed her fluttering lids, whimpering, as the bee tastes the flower waving on a long stem. Now she whispered, "Yes—but first kiss my breasts."

And he did so, his tongue circling in ever smaller arcs till he might teethe like a babe upon the tips. But he was avid now, and moving her about to hold her down with his hands, and quickly she whispered again: "Yes—but first kiss the between of my thighs. Come. Quickly."

And he did so, but he was near violence now, fairly raving as he feasted there, and began to pull on her legs, and grabbed her, and seemed to speak atrocious nonsense, and drove into her, the wanton boy, and fast spilled his foam into her in silly bliss, and collapsed upon her, heavy, and lay there engorged, and at last pulled out of her, and rolled to the side, his breath a whirlwind so she must soothe him, and pull the bedclothes back over him, and stroke his hair and brow and all his head.

"Let me see you," he cried.

But he was exhausted and sinking into sleep, and she whispered, "I have taught you the secret of how to charm a woman. Kiss her eyes. Her breasts. The between of her thighs. Then she must give you anything you ask. Will you remember?"

"Let me see you," he snuffled, already sleeping, and he dreamed of Jetty running home and Quinn standing there asking about his people and his themes. And, in this dream, he answered that he had none and heard all Bri Leith laughing, but he could not find them to stop their laughter, for wherever he turned he saw the damp hills, and the trees, and perhaps Jetty running through. Then he thought he saw himself playing chess with Mistress Firing in a clearing of the woods.

He woke alone, his head aching and his body hungry for company. He thought of the woman of the night, and cursed her for a sore, teasing dream. And he was annoyed to find that the silver crown his ma had given him was gone. Perhaps, in his haste to demonstrate his confidence in the way of the world's doings, he had spent it with Quinn in the pub.

"Whatever the lawyer tells us," Cullin warned his son, "we do the other. Leave him to me, first, to form a judgment on how he'll be treating of us. Then, if it be needed, you'll step in to persuade him."

"I hope it's needed," said Johnny. He'd want a story to take back with him; thus far there was nothing he might properly tell of.

As they walked through Dublin, Johnny saw everything, Cullin only his feet.

"I didn't sleep well," said Cullin. "I don't like having a pile of house atop me, in place of my roof."

"A man can manage in Dublin, da, you said."

"True. But Dublin for some things, Johnny, and Bri Leith for others."

As Cullin worried and Johnny reminisced.

They assumed business posture when they reached the lawyer's office, bluff and tumultuously silent. *Wm. F. MacArt,* the door read, *Solicitor and Legist.* The letters severe. MacArt was hospitable and garrulous, though distracted by the apparatus of his office: maps, licenses, books piled about his desk from foot to waist, and walls of historical renditions, fancifully characterized. *The Defeat at the Boyne, The Crushing of Parnell.* A globe was spinning as they entered.

MacArt seemed to pore over his trove even as he gazed upon his visitors, yet was so intent upon delivering them all of a speedy decision that he found the chance to smile but once in the interview.

"Somewhat, I serve the law of the world," he told them. "Precisely, I uphold the law of the land. In my heart, I observe the law of a people: the law of kind."

"We're very prepared for a lawyer," Cullin began, as danger-
ously as he knew how. Johnny standing by him, tall and cold.

"The passing of a relation," said the solicitor MacArt. "The
fears, the prayer, the contracts. Yes. The next of kin. The youthful,
the aged. The connection and destruction. Yes. Families and death.
Truth, at times it is not the man himself, but his children who
assert his qualities, hold death in check."

Cullin brought out his collection of letters. "Now see," he
began, as the globe came to rest. "We'll have our fair share of it
—here's my lad Johnny to say so."

"Your only child?"

"But he's enough, they say."

"Let's see you, lad."

Johnny did not move.

"He's hale," said MacArt. "A good pair of shoulders on him.
He'll endure."

Johnny put a button on that with a blow, fist to palm.

"He'll whip any man who gives him irritation," Cullin warned.

"Just the one son? Now that Ireland is eating steadily, you owe
the country progeny. Issue. Kind."

"We want what's ours," Cullin whined.

"You shall have it." MacArt took up a file. "It's all before you."
Opening it, spreading papers in repressed excitement. "Lives, pas-
sions. All in print. They say the law is dry, because the law must be
just and justice is heartless. But the law is a history of man. Here's
life in a prospectus." He gave the globe a spin as Johnny glared.
"The law is heartless but man is not. You are not. I am not."

Cullin snorted.

"Nay, sir," said MacArt, the lawyer with the globe. "I wish you
well, and a settlement."

"The terms," Cullin urged.

"The King of Tara had three sons: a warrior, a mason, and a
poet. The warrior died in battle. The poet told lies. But the mason
made the world. It's all in the books."

Johnny strode up to the lawyer's desk to say, "It's now or it's
trouble. What do you give us?"

14

"Your share."

"That is?—and no more of Tara and three sons. I am all the three, Johnny Keogh."

"That is: the principals prefer not to delay settlement with legal action. There are irregularities, contestants, disagreeable questions. But when are there not, where money is to be shared? They have empowered me to assign you a sum down, today, in true money, on the condition that you put your name to a renunciation of all further claims upon the fortune."

"How much?" asked Johnny, still on the edge.

The lawyer handed him an envelope. There was money in it, and a steamship ticket.

"What's this?"

"You wish a quick settlement, and I need a one to deliver something of great value. Something too fine for the post. There's a trade in that, is there not?"

"Deliver where?"

"America."

Cullin, meanwhile, had borrowed the envelope from Johnny and gone through it with satisfaction he could not hide. "However much it is," he announced, "it's not enough."

"So much am I empowered to offer, no more."

"Let it be told," Cullin began, his eyes on Johnny, "that Cullin Keogh—"

"—accepts," Johnny concluded, "and signs."

"I'll not be going to anywhere or America!" cried Cullin.

"No, I'll be the one, da."

"Yes," said the lawyer. "Sometimes a man's history will be told by the deeds of his offspring." As the globe comes to rest again; and then it was that the lawyer smiled.

To celebrate, Johnny and Cullin repaired to The Voyager, where Quinn was elaborating.

"I ask you," says he, "who but a vain man would turn against his own kind, whatever they do? And consider how many kinds a man may have—there's race, religion, county, nation, and fam-

15

ily. There's his obligation of honor and his belief in beauty, his debts and business consociations on the one hand, his romances and friendships on the other. Let a man take too many kinds upon himself all at once—ah! here's the Keoghs, and welcome to your hock!—and he'd be as perplexed to his own principles as a Mayo Protestant singing Italian opera in a Greek synagogue in Chicago, America. Here, what's this package, I wonder?"

"I'll be delivering it to New York for the lawyer."

"What's there inside, do you suppose?"

"He'd not tell us," says Cullin. "Could it be contraband?"

"Papers, he says," Johnny replied. "For the money we get it's worth the while."

"And there you'll be in New York," observed Quinn pensively. "The Dublin of the west."

"I told him," said Cullin, "he ought to find honest work where there is some and then bring his earnings back, to profit his folk."

"A sound advice. But I hear the trip over can be tough enough to deflect most men from trying it twice."

"I will dare," said Johnny, his arm forward and the fists.

"I'm counting on it," said Quinn. "Well, a Tara man in New York. Let's drink on it: to the Irish across the water, and to their fortune, and to fertility!"

"To the Irish!" the other two cried, and the bar rang with echoes and the slap of the hock.

Telling of his Dublin times made Johnny the genius of Bri Leith. "Who owns Ireland?" he asked them down at Murry's, they too spellbound with the theatre of it to think of an answer, so he'd stand even taller and follow up with notes on honor and beauty, and strive with them that they follow the law of kind. So overwhelmed were they, they neglected to ask what kind that might be. He seemed to want to be the superior version of whatever it was the world admired, and preened as he blustered, and joked as he threatened, like an Italian bravo in the old four-volume romances. "I had great events in Dublin," he tells them as Cullin beams nearby without an inkling. "Great events, I say. And who owns Dublin? I did, for the day."

Galloping Toomey named him Dublin Johnny for his trip, and the town went in on it with a hearty grace, except his ma, all of a temper about his going to America. She would burn all ears with her misgivings, then close up like a turtle, silent and still for hours. Is there a town anywhere in Ireland without some memory of a ma who could not bear to be parted from a son, and wept and held him and begged him not to go, and followed his shameful retreat through the streets as if she'd walk after him across the waters? Cullin waltzed about Bri Leith to Murry's and back, but Dublin Johnny saw his mother's look and knew he'd not go easy.

But he would go. Even Jetty, so lovely in her worry and the way she called his name when they met, could not hold him back. She wondered if she should run quite so hard now when he chased her, if he would return as he promised, if he would stay, rather, and send for her, if she would never see him more.

Shall I not have her?, he thought, walking the hills and pondering his dreams at Mistress Firing's. A man who has learned the mastery of women cannot fairly hold himself back ever again. They would look for each other in the afternoons, darker now as the winds came with the stronger rain, and they would have to go inside to talk.

Dublin Johnny would contrive to take Jetty's hand, and whisper to her, and she sensed that he had discovered himself in Dublin, just as was said. It aroused and worried her, as Johnny always had. She looked away as she spoke his name, and he took her face in his hands and gentled her back to see that he was sad. He knew she would not withstand him long, for even before Dublin he had learned that women give special consideration to a man who will show them a little sorrow. And of course now, after Dublin, he had a city smile to show her, too.

And so it happened that he walked over one day, asking her to mend his coat, for there was a small rip in the lining. And for him to apply to Jetty and not his ma was a notable thing. Luckily Mary was not about then, or none of this could occur.

Dublin Johnny sat in the main room of the house as Jetty examined the coat, a great monstrous rough handsome thing like her Johnny, a proud coat, and he thrown across a chair smiling at her. Then he came over.

"If you would mend it," he began softly.

"I will. So it will keep you as warm on your trip home as going away."

He nodded, eyes full on her.

"You will come home, then?"

"I suppose I have the reason to. Do I, lady?" Slipping onto the bench next to her.

"I'll get my things," she answered, dropping her gaze. For a moment, she did not move—then bolted into the bedroom with the coat to find a needle and thread. And when she turned back, he was in the doorway and not smiling, and she thought, If I give too much, I lose him. But he was close by her then, his head back and looking down at her. "Do you not want me after all?" he said.

"I love you, Johnny."

"Then let me see you."

She shook her head.

"Let me see you if you love me, Jetty."

"I'll love you married, Johnny Keogh."

"Dublin Johnny Keogh." He took her by the waist. "You'll love me now."

"That'll be enough of that," she said, pushing him away, "and Mary home any minute from this. Wasn't it your coat I'm mending, then?"

"Won't you kiss me, Jetty?" Stroking her hair. "You've kissed me often before." Preparing to charm her, thinking of it. "Here I am soon away for a certain time. We'll miss each other. Kiss me, Jetty, and let me see you. Will I hurt you, little one? Is that what you think?" He seemed offended, amazed; but to say they won't hurt you if you will is meant to remind you they will hurt you if you don't. "You think I'll hurt you?"

She touched him. Jaw. Mouth. Hair. "I love you, Johnny. I'll wait and you'll come back and we'll marry."

"Dublin Johnny," he insists, but his hands are in his pockets, his shoulders drawn down. "Can't you trust me?" The dread faker.

18

Turned away so she can't see him getting hard to charm a woman. "I've dreamed of seeing you, Jetty. I saw you lying still before me, and you were so trusting. I need you to trust me, darling." She put out a hand to him, touched his back. He looks. It's near the time. "I only wish to show you how I feel about you, Jetty." His arms about her, the devil. "Jetty." She drops the coat upon the floor, buries her face in his chest as he rubs her neck.

"Yes," he says. "Jetty," he says. "Darling."

"Johnny, I long for you, but we—"

"Let me see you if you trust me."

"Please, Johnny."

"Do you trust me?"

Kissing her eyes.

She speaks his name over and over as he smoothly unlaces her, bends her, moves her. He has a few secrets of his own from before Dublin: go slow and murmur romantic blackmail. Don't you trust me? Can't you like me? Would you make me sad enough to need to hurt you? Did not the King of Tara wrestle with the fairy Bala na Killahee for five days and nights before he pinned her to earth? "The demon a man!" the fairy Bala is believed to have cried out then, "for they make us fire so we will them on to burn!"

Kissing her breasts; and she weeps, knowing what must come, moaning his name, and "please," and his name. He has her on the bed, out of her shift, helpless, and as she attempts to rise he catches her up with such insistent tenderness that she gives up all resistance when he forces her down.

Kissing the between of her thighs, and she is his.

Her eyes close as he strokes her, her arms limp.

"I love to see you so," he says. "And hear you plead with me. To see you, Jetty." His finger prowls up the length of her to her chin and he presses upon her arms to kiss her eyes again. She cries out, strains against him, and he shakes his head at her, smiling, for he has charmed her, and she can no more escape than fly to Wight.

Then the bedroom door bangs open, a shaft of light slashes at them through the darkness, and Mary stands in the doorway, her eyes like ash and a broom in her hands, held where the wood bites the straw, the handle upraised.

Johnny leaps up.

"The he-witch!" cries Mary, smashing Johnny across the face with the wood of the broom, hard. *"Get you behind!"*

He goes for her, but she wields the broom as the Hag of Sligo berated the Giant McKinnafee when he broke into her candy garden: and, we recall, he was not seen again in Sligo for four centuries after.

Never had Johnny glimpsed such a look on a woman's face, not even his ma's. The blows came so fast that he had no choice but to flee; what would he get if he stayed, at that, but screams and the shameful beating of a woman? He ran, Mary whacking at him through the house as if she hoped to kill him, and she bolts the door after him, throws down the broom, and comes back into the bedroom.

Fearful of her sister's anger, and distraught in her Jezebel nakedness, Jetty hadn't moved, and stayed so even when Mary stood over her, an outline in the dim light spilling through the doorway, cool as ever and sure of the morality of the case. At any rate Jetty had the sense of occasion to turn her face away.

"And him days away from his trip," said Mary at last.

"I'm afraid to lose him, Mary," cried Jetty. "I'm afraid he'll not come back." Again she wept.

"Is this the way to keep in his thoughts? So?"

"He brought his coat to mend, and followed me here . . . oh, Mary, the . . . the touch of him!" She heaved with sobs as Mary knelt for something at her feet.

"What's this?" Mary asked, holding it.

"His coat, I'm telling you. Give it me, why don't you, to cover myself with, at least."

Instead, Mary brought the kit to the bed and fished out the scissors. "If you had any brains at all," she muttered, looming over her sister with the scissors.

"Mary!"

"Hold still."

With great care, Mary cut away a bit of her sister's Venus hair.

"Now," said Mary, "and stop gaping: hand me the coat and the needle, and we'll see how to keep his mind on you while he's over."

As Jetty looked on, Mary sewed the hairs into the lining of the coat.

"But, Mary—"

"This is making the magic," said Mary evenly, "to fetch him back. Tomorrow, you'll bring him his coat. A night without it won't hurt the likes of him." Mary finished off the stitching, tore the thread to stay. "It's not the chill that bothers that man. It's warmth."

Walk into New York and ask for a Mr. O'Faoire and give him the package. Papers, he says, and that they are: many kinds, and colors, and sizes. Some handwritten, it seems, and some printed by some artisan very pleasing with his tricks. Lovely etchings on some, little portraits.

"Here are letters of bond and repudiation," says Mr. O'Faoire, "and agreements of limited time." Johnny waiting for a receipt, shifting his feet. He does not smile; why waste it on a man? "Here's one telling of a lonely man who would greet the world again, could it be arranged," says Mr. O'Faoire in his office, Dublin Johnny there in his coat with his eyes cold. He had come straight from the boat, walked into New York. "Here's a mother longing for her son, to see him a last time. Or contracts. Here, this, between two brothers starting up a consortium for the prevention of the spread of despair among the Irish urban poor."

"I want to go now," said Johnny. "Give me a receipt."

"Why? You'll not see MacArt again."

It sounded right but felt wrong. Challenged, Dublin Johnny fell back on ancient routine. "I'll see what I like," he snarled, "and take a receipt for delivery."

"Well, then," writing something, folding it too much and slowly, handing it there, and smiling so broadly that Dublin Johnny feels foolish and runs out of the place. He feels worse in the hall, so he steps back, opens the lawyer's door, and slams it hard: his punctua-

tion. On the marbled glass one reads, *O'Faoire, The Connector.*
Dublin Johnny starts off into New York, his new place, in his coat.

New York is a different kind than Dublin, silver, black, and
crowded. Many of the people seem to have nowhere to go, dully
wandering. Others trot, suggesting great affairs in train. Ah, Bri
Leith is over, Dublin Johnny tells himself, even as he feels home-
sick, and turns himself in some direction that might be home,
wondering at it. Jetty.

The receipt, when he thinks to unfold and examine it, is no
receipt at all, but a bill advertising a guest house for home folk,
on which O'Faoire wrote, "Miss Nora will see to you." Well,
Dublin Johnny did as he promised, anyway, did he not? And, true,
he never will see MacArt again, will he?

Miss Nora is red, fast, and candid, and says, as she shows Dublin
Johnny the room, "The gentleman is appreciative of the advantages of a clean and respectable establishment. He wonders about
the quality of the household sociability."

"Am I?" Dublin Johnny replies.

She raises her right index finger in mock warning.

"I'll not be stopping long," says Dublin Johnny.

"The gentleman knows his mind, but not his way." She opens
a window, looking on the street filled with the folk of a hundred
places. "Everything changes here."

Nora, too, has an older sister, but Miss Molleen is as gentle as
an infant. She appears enthusiastic and doubtful at once, as if she
feared that her closest associates might deny her everything wonderful at any moment. The main thing she says is, "How will you
take your tea?"

"Sweet and boiling," Dublin Johnny replies, looking at Nora.

Nora smiles. "What'll you be up to here?" she says. "The lady
asks."

"I'll find work."

Molleen, unseeing, reports that Uncle Flaherty would be hiring
a man, part of the time, you understand, on the Forty-eighth Street

project. An office building going up. They're short hands there. As Nora and Dublin Johnny exchange shrugs and grins.

It seems good.

Dublin Johnny moves in and sees about being an extra hand on Forty-eighth Street. It's out of the union, you understand. Off the book. Still, they can always find room for an Irishman.

Nora walking about, not looking.

For there's certain things that belong to the Irish here, certain jobs.

Dublin Johnny's eyes following her.

Certain ways of living. For instance, you'll notice that in Ireland most folk live out on the green. Whereas here in America the Irish live in cities.

Nora finds a bit of dust on a windowsill. No good but that she'll clean it just now, clean it for the guest, the Dublin Johnny, and his jaw and his smile and the way he moves in.

We all must marry at a time. Some of us marry a friend, some a stranger.

"I'll marry a sweetheart," says Nora. "Whispers and dancing."

"Esh," cries Molleen. "What'll you have, Nora, in the end?"

"Him."

And she knows. She counts off a certain number of days, marked by evenings along the pier, in the park, on a roof. Taking his tea up to his room when he drags back from Forty-eighth Street. Playing him music on the Victrola, while Molleen can't imagine what the two of them are laughing at.

At last Nora offers to mend Dublin Johnny's coat.

"It doesn't need mending, lady."

"Sure, a coat always needs. As you've only the one. . . ."

"It's *my* one," he replies, everything a quiz or a war.

"All the more yours," she urges, "after it's mended new."

He takes it up, weighs it, thinking. He looks at Nora and sees Jetty.

"He gives it over," says Nora, so still.

And he does.

She takes it into her room, and searches the lining for the stitching, over and over in a ma's needle track—but see! *There* is the one she wants, one tuft of thread set in an alien hand.

Nora rips at the threading and pulls out the hairs.

Nora touches the spot where they were with her finger, kisses it, touches the spot again.

"So," she purrs.

PART TWO

The Princes of Tara
Come into Their History

The Story of

GREAT AMERICAN JOHNNY

When he had a case of the whispers, he would sneak away from them and talk it out with himself, planning revenges. There was little he could do against the grown-ups, the little one, no matter how big—because angry—he felt, except perhaps beat up his younger brother Mike, to hurt his ma. She loved Mike too special not to be hurt. It was funny how you could actually see them all taking in the special love of hers for Mike, noticing it and getting quiet and thinking about it, how it was wrong and they all knew it. But they never said anything about it, did they? They never told her to be nice to all her children; and did they ever take him in their laps and pet him the way they did Mike? Sure, they didn't.

"Your father was so proud of you when you were born," they were always telling him. His first son. There's no drunk, they say, like the drunk of an Irishman turning father to his first boy in America, but Dublin Johnny broke all the records even so. As Uncle Flaherty told it, trying to cheer young Johnny when his da seemed to accuse him of not being all that a man should be in the deft jabs and joking that win friends to your side, Dublin Johnny began his round of the pubs the very moment Molleen had taken Nora to the hospital, and he did not spare the barkeep's arm till news arrived that Nora had brought home a boy. By then, Dublin Johnny could only be called a creature at war with his innards: they were determined to throw him off his feet and sleep off the flood of beer inside a quiet man; he was just as determined to hold standing, and go on babbling and musing and striking off incoherent verse to the honor of his people.

Finally, escorted home by a group of his friends under the shadow of the Third Avenue El, Dublin Johnny stopped fast, cried out, "Now I give Tara its prince!", reeled, and landed in their arms. And so they brought him home to his wife and babe. Just how long Dublin Johnny had maintained his state of inebriation is unknown, for he was already a good half the cask ahead of the world when he showed up at Clancy's, where his friends gathered. But all the neighborhood has agreed it was the grandest wet bash-up in any memory, and became known as The Long Drunk of Dublin Johnny Keogh.

Young Johnny liked the story, the only thing about his father he did like. According to Uncle Flaherty, Dublin Johnny doted on his infant strenuously, walking him about the parlor from the Victrola to the davenport, and sliding down the stairs for a sport with the boy in his lap till Nora had to take the child away from him for fear he'd get broken. When Johnny got the whispers about his father and had to figure out what to do about him, he would try to recall this part of his life, but could not visualize Dublin Johnny playing with him. Cuffing him for not smiling the Keogh grin: that he remembered. Scuffling him about for having a bitter look in his eyes: oh yes. Telling him to be smart or he'd not be the Great American Johnny that any Dublin John Keogh, Jr. ought to be: this, too. But no father that Johnny knew of had ever played with him.

It was odd how grown-ups told different stories about the same things. Uncle Flaherty's versions of the past had a friendly, expansive quality, like the tales the men told each other in saloons, with a flavor of invention about them, as if each telling discovered new details. Aunt Molleen's accounts were more confidential, more forgiving, and came out in tiny eruptions separated by hesitant longings. When she told of Dublin Johnny's Long Drunk, Nora came forward as the principal figure, the men and their beery meanderings a background to the suffering of the childbed.

"She was there a while for you, Johnny," Aunt Molleen would tell him. "A great while at it, and crying so long I feared she'd dry up altogether. She hardly saw you when you came and they gave you to her, to feel of you and know you." She would stop here, seem to scan the scene in some private picture album of the past, to be sure she had it right. "Your father wanted her to lie in at home in the old form of it, but your mother was born on American land, and she would have her way and the hospital doctors, if only for the one night. Esh, the strange bed. The strange people running about."

"Who was there?" Johnny asked her once.

"Your mother and her sister Molleen and you." She nodded. "Us three."

This, in a misty way, Johnny seemed to recall. He saw it. "To feel of me," he often whispered, brooding, "and know me." Sometimes, when he was really mad at everyone and had been off whispering for hours, it was this sight of Nora in the strange hospital bed that finally drew him back to the guest house where they all lived, and he would find Nora in the kitchen and sit watching her sew or cook or talk to Aunt Molleen. They would pat him and he would nod, a replica of Dublin Johnny with someone not at all like Dublin Johnny inside him, someone who had no yen to smile, Great American Johnny as still and silent as a mousetrap.

Anyone seemed closer to him than his da, so loud and unruly, darting about him with hits at his arms to make him fight and be tough, or coming home floating in after-work beer, bellowing as he stumbled into Johnny's room to wake him and make him play with his miniature tool box. Was this what it was like when Johnny was a baby and his da played with him? And when he went to his ma to be comforted, she'd have her mind on other things. "He's your da," she'd say, all she'd say.

Sometimes she walked Johnny over to Dublin Johnny's site, wherever it was, for the neighborhood was undergoing Reevaluation in those early Eisenhower years, and many buildings were coming down so bigger ones could rise in their place. Dublin Johnny was in the ironworkers' union now, thanks to Uncle Flaherty, and perhaps they all thought Johnny would be impressed by the size of the work, and Dublin Johnny in his metal hat and suspenders and boots, and all the men with him, slapping each other and looking like there was plenty they'd say of Nora if Dublin Johnny wasn't around. Johnny hated these trips, and took to making Nora promise him they'd walk somewhere else, though he was afraid that then she might not walk with him at all.

Aunt Molleen was nice to him, and Uncle Flaherty gave him kind words. But of all in the house, the only one Johnny really felt comfortable with was one of the boarders, an Italian man with a very gentle way, unlike the men Johnny was related to. The Italian man had a night job, so he was often in in the daytime, to visit in the parlor while Aunt Molleen went over the accounts and Nora played records. Johnny would settle into the Italian man's lap and listen to tales of the old days, when strangers asked each other riddles at the drop of a hat, and to fail to answer might be fatal; and when witches fooled kings and destroyed kingdoms, calling it only mischief and pranks; and when handsome princes did smite their foes or died young. Sometimes both. The Italian man told a bold story, and Aunt Molleen and Nora would listen as faithfully as Johnny, though Nora might dance through the room at certain points, as if enacting the lovely princess in distress that the Italian man's stories always featured.

Once Johnny told Aunt Molleen he wished the Italian man could be his father instead of Dublin Johnny. "Esh, don't go saying such things!" cried Aunt Molleen. "What if Saint Patrick hears you?"

"What would happen?"

Aunt Molleen shook her head. "Child, I hardly know. But rash

30

things occur when you start wishing for a different life. Best leave things as they are, now."

"I hope he does hear me."

Johnny tried whispering to Saint Patrick, begging him to smite Johnny's many foes, but nothing came of it. When I'm older, Johnny thought, I will smite them myself. He had seen, one Saturday night, two policemen drag a man into the street outside the guest house, throw him against a parked car, and beat him. Aunt Molleen found Johnny watching at his window, and tried to take him away, but he fought her savagely. He wanted to see how to smite a man.

The Italian man came there, too, attracted by the noise, and wondered at the fury of the policemen, to treat a person of the town so brutally before his fellow citizens, all at their windows, watching.

"He deserves it," said Nora, coming up close to the Italian man, and watching him rather than the beating of the man in the street. "He comes home like a sot to scream at his wife and make her terrified, and beats her, too, the animal. And for nothing. How often have they come, the policemen, summoned by her neighbors. And what? They arrest him, and once he is out of jail he is back to beat her again."

Johnny watched her watching the Italian man.

"Now," said Nora, "they will make an example of him not to be so bitter to his wife."

"Esh," said Aunt Molleen, in the farthest corner from the window. "It doesn't look right for the neighborhood."

"The guest would enjoy a cup of something hot," said Nora. "Coffee, maybe?"

Yes, please, he would.

"Esh," said Aunt Molleen, when they had gone, and she would go on but could not say what she had in mind to Nora's own son.

Johnny thought he knew, anyway. He looked hard at Aunt Molleen. "Does da beat ma like that man? Would the policemen come?"

"Whssht. The crafty boy!"

31

"Then could ma marry the Italian man?"

"Mary and Joseph!"

"Well, da marries other women, doesn't he? He is out marrying one now."

Aunt Molleen put a hand to her gaping mouth.

"Uncle Flaherty knows. I heard him talking of it to da. Uncle Flaherty says I can marry lots of girls when I've the age for it. He says it's in the blood. He says da is a natural lady biter. He doesn't bite them, though, does he? I saw ma kiss the Italian man."

Aunt Molleen began to cry.

"When I was whispering, once. I saw them. Is the Italian man a lady biter, too?"

He sat down and watched Aunt Molleen weep. If she tried to make him go to bed, he decided, he'd scare her with the mouse he caught. Sometimes he dropped them out of his window and sometimes he put them in a box to die by themselves.

When Nora brought her second child home from the hospital, Johnny felt neglected by grown-ups for the first time he could recall. Normally they fussed at him with *no!* and *later!* Now, suddenly, they ignored him to coo over his baby brother, named Parnell Michael. This time Nora had had an easy birth—or, as no birth is easy, easier than many and much easier than Johnny's had been. So, of course, they were glad to tell him a hundred times. Dublin Johnny had scarce got a roll in his legs and a buzz in his ears before it was time, and he trooped home with his friends to admire the new one, and roar laughing, and shout songs, and make a commotion.

No one said a word to Johnny—the Italian man would have, sure, but he was gone by then. So Johnny went to his room and brought back his tool chest, a miniature of the grown-up's kit, with hammer, wrench, ruler, nails, and such. Johnny tried strolling through the room with his articles; still no one cared to admire him. Then it occurred to him to demonstrate the power of the instruments, so he pulled out the hammer and went to the baby

to pound its little head; but Aunt Molleen read his plan and
snatched the hammer from him, and hit his nose.

"Did you see the Johnny?" his da cried. "He's the warrior of
the family, sure!"

Nora said nothing, but her look burned Johnny's face, and he
took himself away to whisper.

A great frustration of those years was the discovery that babies are
not afraid of mice, but a great liberty then was the neighborhood,
with its streets of trouble and subterfuge. Johnny was the youngest
member of his gang, the Fifty-fifth Street Brigade, but he often
directed their exploits, especially in the harassing of the fancy
people moving into the new high-rise buildings along the river.
One of them went up next to the guest house, and Aunt Molleen
and Nora had actually been offered a sum by developers closing
in on a site.

Johnny was a daredevil, always seeking a ruthless new height
from which to leap into the river, attended by the usual witnesses
and Gilda Bono, who had given him a valentine and who could be
counted on to scream in apparently unsimulated terror at the
moment of the leap. It was usual, in swimming stunts, to lure one's
comrades into coming along by threatening to call them cowards
if they didn't. The aim of a group dive was partly reassurance—
danger loves company—and partly cheap bravado, for a few always chickened out, adding to the glory of those who dared. But
Johnny never asked anyone to come along with him. At times, he
seemed to regard the gang not as playmates or confederates but as
messengers or sources of alibi. For as he grew older he became not
wiser or gentler, just bigger and stronger. He looked even more
like his father than before, yet seemed less like him than ever. And
Johnny knew it, for the difference was hard to miss, his da so
casually responsive to a joke or compliment and so tenacious with
the ladies, the boy always wondering what was on another's mind,
and as gloomy with women as with men. Nor did they sound alike,
for Dublin Johnny had not only retained his brogue but expanded
it, as if serving Tara in some ambassadorial venture, while Johnny

spoke the pure New York of the streets, making it difficult now to narrate his saga in the notable ancient style. And, as Dublin Johnny had grown yet somewhat distant from Nora, as a man will after years of marriage, so had Johnny grown closer to her: or tried to. But he felt her seeing the father when she looked at the son. It was Mike she loved to see. She laughed like someone you might hear on the radio, just to watch the infant hauling himself along the furniture, and the day he walked unaided she wept for joy.

All those rituals of childhood, from measles to confirmation, Nora celebrated with Mike as she hadn't with Johnny. Why? Because Mike was specially hers? It did Johnny no good to punish Mike for being special, either. For if Nora caught him at it, she would get fierce and hard and not speak to Johnny for weeks after, leaving Aunt Molleen to retain the child in the household sociability.

One night Aunt Molleen came into Johnny's room carrying the new baby, Dennis, and asked Johnny if he'd like to hold him. Johnny sat carefully on the edge of the bed and rocked the infant, Aunt Molleen superintending close next to him. The baby smiled at Johnny and wrapped its tiny hand around his finger.

"This one likes me," said Johnny. "Dennis likes me."

"You must be patient with your family, child," Aunt Molleen blurted out, a little shocked at her own frankness. "Everyone means well, now, but they don't always make the best of it. You see, Johnny?"

Johnny hummed a lullaby and rocked the baby.

"It's not right for your poor ma, with your da so often away, and she not knowing whether he's dead in the gutter or drinking health with his friends. Will you be patient, then? Your ma was always strange in her ways of showing love, even when she was a girl."

Johnny began to improvise lyrics in a ragged chant, more exhaling than singing:

> *Sleep, baby,*
> *Rocking dear,*
> *Mike is dead*
> *And Johnny's here.*

Aunt Molleen patted his arm. "That's right. We all find our ways of showing love, different . . . different for each person we love, isn't it? Your ma has a way for me, and one for your uncle, and one for your da . . . and then you, and Parnell Michael, and the wee new one here."

Johnny was humming.

"All the people are different in the family. All of us make different mistakes. There's a lot of forgiving to do, Johnny."

The baby fell asleep with his hand clutching Johnny's finger.

"This one likes me," he said.

There was a photograph taken on July 4, 1961 on the New Jersey shore, whither the entire Flaherty-Keogh clan repaired for a vacation on funds drawn from the sale of the guest house. Nora, imperious, stands next to Dublin Johnny, his arm around her waist and his smile seizing the camera; but his eyes are travelling, as if something distracted them the moment the shutter snapped. Molleen is trying to look wickedly captivating, her head aimed at Uncle Flaherty's shoulder. He is disapproving and tolerant.

The children, smiling without nuance, stand before the adults: Johnny, a few months short of thirteen, with his hands on the shoulders of eight-year-old Dennis, and Mike, ten then, near his great-uncle. The brisk black-and-white of the boardwalk photographer fails to capture the red and green of Nora, the soft browns and pinks of the Keoghs, but it emphasizes Mike's dark coloring, jauntily tanned and set as it is against the uniform fairness of the others. He might be a friend, a distant cousin.

Who of us doesn't appreciate a family photograph—so public a presentation, yet so confidential? Here is all the world of feelings at once, with its caring, and silly humors, and contentious, teeming needs trimmed in clammy smiles, a collection of scandals pretending not to happen. Had this picture been taken at the end of the vacation instead of at the start, Dennis would have been standing with Mike, not Johnny, and that would be the truer portrait of the three sons of Dublin Johnny Keogh: for it was on the shore that the troubles broke out among them. Not *began*, I tell, for there was trouble between Johnny and Mike from Mike's birth, and Johnny's moody bearing often disrupted his relations with Dennis. But there is this, essentially: that some of us are holding people and some of us are held people; and Johnny had been holding Dennis since he had been an infant, singing to him and telling him tales of his army of mice who assembled upon a secret command, and of the tunnel demons who used to nab their prey under the Third Avenue El before they tore it down, and of Tara, of course—but those were Dublin Johnny's tales, and Johnny preferred his own. They were surely too vivid for Dennis, for when he was very young he would become frightened and not want to hear them out, and Johnny would wax angry with him, and hold him fast and make him hear, even if he was crying.

So there is this as well: that some of the holding people are vexatious about it, and blunt, and if you try to elude their grasp they will call their army of mice down upon you. And while it may be true that love is stronger than anger, fear is stronger than love. And, though neither of them knew it, Dennis was learning to fear Johnny.

At the time of the photograph, all was well with the family, perhaps especially with Aunt Molleen, who would lark about under her little sun parasol and then stagger back to the accommodations feeling "all of a dizzy." Even Dublin Johnny, so seldom about the guest house when there were beautiful women to charm, played husband on this trip, lolling on the sand with his Nora and teasing her till she blushed. And Johnny taught Dennis how to swim, and Dennis loved the water, and all three boys played together as brothers should, dunking each other and shouting as they ran along the breakwaters.

Sometimes the smallest thing can shatter the peace. Johnny came down to the water one morning to find Mike showing Dennis refinements in the aquatic arts, the two of them splashing and holding each other and laughing the way Johnny and Dennis did. Shaking off the whispers, Johnny crashed into the surf, yelling incoherently. But what words can one put to the thought, This one likes *me*, not you? Who assigns rights to teaching little brothers to swim? Who owns? Who holds? But Dennis looked guilty, as if he had indeed assigned such rights, and to Johnny. And Mike got tense, as he always did when Johnny found him crossing one of Johnny's barriers.

On land, Johnny would have fought them both, but the water slowed everyone, so more curses were exchanged than blows. At last, frustrated and raw, feeling the anger billowing in him as the foul haunts flap above Devil's Bog, Johnny took himself away in a bad black silence. What he knew for certain was that this time Dennis was the bad one, not Mike. Dennis was the one; Dennis had said he liked Johnny, as good as said it.

The smallest thing, then: but it did not feel small to Johnny. For some days after, he would not speak to Dennis, would not even glance at him. He stared Aunt Molleen down when she came to him on the porch one evening after dinner and asked him to tell her what was wrong, and why he would not be kind to Dennis, his own flesh, and so dependent upon him, and esh, this family of sinners, and we are all sinners—this last is not wisdom, but the Church only, speaking its ironclad prattle through the head of one of its most impressionable daughters. Yet it is true that this is a family of sinners, of secrets kept and shared. Each of them will bear his set; and each, I fear, will act harshly to his own kind. Yet, if I may pass on any lesson at all to my readers, it is that they must treat their own sort gently, and others, too, and that they be ready, when it is time, to assume a great forgiving tenderness; and ask it as well.

Aunt Molleen might have said as much to Johnny on the porch of their vacation place on the only extended holiday the clan ever took. But there was no beseeching that gritty heart, and Dennis held distant from Johnny, becoming closer by the hour with the genial, tolerant Mike, who did not believe in armies of mice. And Johnny saw this, and nourished his rage as Dennis innocently multiplied his crimes.

Then, near the end of the vacation, Dennis thought to make things up with Johnny, and came rollicking into the ocean, into the deep where Johnny was bobbing on the waves. Johnny ignored Dennis' calls, so Dennis thought it might be a neat prank to give

37

Johnny a dunking, and leaped upon his back. But Johnny threw him off and, catching him about the arms, hissed that Dennis would be sorry now, you dirty little cheat, and thrust him under the water, and held him there, and caught him by the legs, too, to stop his struggling, and Dennis was drowning.

A stranger, taking this for a childish game getting out of hand, pulled them apart. And when Dennis came up, vomiting water, his body heaving, he did not flee Johnny, but reached for him, in confusion, as if begging him to say it was an accident, or that a mysterious power had taken possession of him to inspire him to such a wicked act. But it was Johnny who had done it, Johnny willing, and Johnny whom Dennis touched, Johnny unforgiving, so easily wounded and so quick to strike.

The family came back to New York and closed up the guest house, moving to separate quarters in the neighborhood. Aunt Molleen claimed a floor-through on Fiftieth Street, Uncle Flaherty two rooms around the corner of First Avenue, and the Keoghs the top floor of a brownstone on Fifty-fourth Street. Now the three boys must share a room, but they held to the pattern developed on the beach, Dennis and Mike in one corner, Johnny in the opposite corner. Yet Johnny hung a copy of the boardwalk photograph on the wall of the boys' bedroom. Mike never looked at it, but Dennis would climb on the bed to study it. One day, a year after the picture was taken, Johnny came in, saw Dennis there, slipped behind him, and grabbed him for a joke. But Dennis, startled, fell backward onto the floor and hurt his head.

"Why did you do that?" he cried.

"I didn't," Johnny told him. "It happened."

Mike came in.

"I was joking," said Johnny.

"Oh yes?" Dennis got behind Mike. "Well, you're always joking. And then someone falls off or gets cut."

"I was just—"

"And at the beach you held me under the water and I almost got drowned!" Dennis ran out.

"Really neat," said Mike.

38

"Shut up!"

"Oh yeah?"

The three-year difference in their ages is dangerous at that era, for each year means a significant increase in bone and muscle. Johnny was well over six feet then, and heavy, and wild. And he had never liked Mike. He had been waiting for a chance to show him how he felt about him. But, as he went up to Mike, Dennis suddenly returned, hovering in the doorway.

"Stop being so mean to us!" Dennis shouted.

Music crawled down the hall from Nora's Victrola.

"Who's *us?*" asked Johnny.

Dennis was behind Mike again.

"Us is the world," said Mike.

Johnny socked him. Mike stood there. Johnny socked him harder. Mike socked him back. Then, as Johnny threw himself on Mike, screaming for joy, Dennis jumped in, pummelling Johnny's head and shouting something. Mike fought valiantly, but he was frankly overmatched and Johnny pinned him, bending his arm behind his back. "Give in or I'll break it," he said.

"How long do you think you can push us around?" said Mike, panting but cool, a child who will be a conclusive man. "We've put up with it, but from now on . . . "

Johnny forced the arm and Mike cried out despite himself, and Dennis was suddenly there, petting Johnny and saying, "Don't hurt him anymore. It was our fight. Don't hurt him." Slowly Johnny let go of Mike, and let him up, and watched him lead Dennis out of the room, and remembered what Dennis had shouted: *"We hate you!"*

Who's *we?* he whispered very late that night, on a bench in the new park they erected where the FDR Drive pulls into Fifty-third Street. After all this, who's we?

"Man with the gift can't keep his hands still," muttered a baglady a few inches to Johnny's north. "Think God sent them to cheer us. Know what cheers me? A joker. I like a man who makes me laugh."

Johnny stared at her.

"Don't waste it on me, young feller. Plenty of damsels to take you up. Give me a joker and my *Coronet*. I have to do my piece of reading. Keep up. Like a good story better than I like a man. Fumblers can hardly get to amen on you, and the varsity, well . . . they believe they're discovering America. But they can't hold back when they think they've got a lady's number. When they think they'll charm her. You in the Church?"

Johnny grunted.

"Sure. Well, baptizing won't get you into any party I know of. That's not the ticket, and you know it, pretty boy like you. Big boy, big shoulders. I see you. I see you. Where you from? Something I can do for you?"

Johnny shook his head.

"Talk, don't you?"

Nothing. Whispers in his head. Go, lady.

"Bet you're in the Church. Silent men always are. Don't I know?" She opened her blouse. "Don't I know about baptized men? Circumscribed men in the Church? Don't I?"

Johnny leaned toward her.

"Your father's a whore. What does that make you?"

Johnny sucked on her breasts.

"Not my fault if someone saw. Your father, your uncle. They're all drunken whores. Try lower down, no one's here." He looked up and saw a gun in her hand. "Found it." She spun the barrel. "Loaded, too. I'll bet you like this. What's your name, tender?"

He took the gun from her.

"What's your name, I tell you?"

He aimed the gun at her head.

"Course, who am I to say what it is? I don't know about it. I can hold back. Policeman, nothing, I don't *know* it, you know?"

In the winter, all three boys in the same bed, they would pile up like puppies to get warm. But they did not speak. Sometimes Johnny would say goodnight to Dennis, with his name on it so, to effect peace, and sometimes Nora would come by to bid them all sweet dreams in a tone meant for Mike only. Sometimes also they heard Dublin Johnny crash in at any hour, and let Nora's chastenings befuddle him; or not let, and shove past her with a roar as if he meant to wreck the house. Sometimes, when he heard Dennis breathing in the vulnerability of sleep, Johnny would take hold of him, and Dennis would hold him back and murmur: "Can I come along with you?"

"There was no Church in Tara," Dublin Johnny told Father Doyle. "There was men and witches."

"God listens, you Keogh!"

"Not to you, mollycoddle priester," said Dublin Johnny.

A much-quoted neighborhood incident. Yet, in the family, only Aunt Molleen took mind. Truth to tell, she was one of your errant churchgoers, as afraid of the Christian epic as impressed by it. There was too much blood in Christ for her taste, she said. Still, she wailed that war between the Father and the parishioners could only lead to scuffles. As she drank her tea. As Uncle Flaherty sat beside, on a visit, always a plain man who never liked anything but his work, making buildings go up. As Dennis stood close to Mike and Nora smiled like a queen. To confound Johnny, she called Dennis little boy; and Mike called Dennis little brother; and Dennis called him Iron Mike; and they would all look at Johnny when he came in a room as if he had no name at all.

"Look who," says Nora.

"We'll all be nice," says Aunt Molleen, fluttery.

I have a gun in a secret place.

"Your da hates the Father," says Nora. "The news."

"Cursing all priests," Uncle Flaherty puts in. "Eunuchs telling us how to live."

"Blasphemy," says Nora, relishing it. "Young Johnny, come and sit." She pats a cushion. "She wonders how much he knows and tells."

Johnny ignores this.

"The way to my heart," she observes, "is to love your brother Parnell Michael. Protect him. Foster him. If you love me, Johnny."

They played Spook, wherein the lights are put out and one of the company, chosen by cards but unknown to the others, claims a victim in the dark with a kiss. Lights on, all must guess who did it. First round, Uncle Flaherty murdered Aunt Molleen, and who could not guess as much from her pestering giggles? Second round, Nora murdered Mike, and it was hard to say who guessed it least fast. In the third round, a fight broke out, and the lights came up on Nora blazing at Johnny, as if she'd known he'd go for Mike with no kiss in mind.

"Is that it?" she cried. "Is it?"

"Yeah, that's it," said Johnny.

"So."

"That's it."

And that damn Dennis standing with Mike again. How does that happen? We hate you. Your father is a drunken whore. Can I come along with you? Ma and the Italian man were drinking coffee downstairs. Young Johnny was babbling in a confessional in a strange parish in a remote part of the town, one of those all-night services planned for sinners so convulsed by their errors that they must hasten into the booth and purge the collected guilt so they may start out again and pay their greed for fresh atrocities. How does that happen, Father? Make them be kinder to me, and I will be kind.

The Father droned out a recipe of penances.

The little one liked me first.

Go my son, the Father yawns.

Johnny stole out of the stupid church, exhausted by anger, whispering. What terrible thing can I do?

The city is black, furtive characters scuttling up the street as Johnny approaches. Distant laughter, a slap, a bottle falls and smashes. A man in grand attire weaves down Twenty-fourth Street, drunk. He pauses, puts a hand to his head, totters, stands. He sees Johnny. As Johnny strides past him the man lurches into him and bounces a few paces back.

"Why don't you . . . ?" he slurs. ". . . where you're walking? Bump into . . . into decent people . . . ?"

"You fucking jerk!" Johnny hisses.

The man looks into Johnny's face to tremble. Looking for it. "*You* look!" Johnny tells him. "Why don't *you* look?"

The man hands Johnny his billfold.

"Take it," he whines. "Leave me . . . helpless." Enjoying himself, maybe. "You're a roughneck of the streets, capable of anything." He lurches again. "So ruthless."

The billfold is thick.

"Please," says the man. "Please, please, please, please, please, please, please."

"Please what, you?"

"Do . . . what you will."

Jonny stares at the man, takes a few steps, turns and stares again, moves on.

"*I won't tell anyone!*" the man hollers.

The baglady nodded when Johnny showed her the billfold. "One of those rich ones? Money to spare. See, what I do: I go to their banquets and spit in the food." She trilled laughter. "Did you use the gun on him?"

Johnny gazed upon the lights of the Fifty-ninth Street Bridge.

"All they can understand. Force of arms." She aimed a finger and shot at a garbage scow gliding down to open sea. "Plenty more rich ones, too. Easy picking. City's full of them. Show them the gun, call it charity tax. Blessing in costume. Holy war. Better than going around drunk and seductive like your father. That charm's a killer. Makes a man weak. Makes him love a lady till his head's empty. Keep at it all night, blood's like cake frosting, brains like a cracker. Think they're in heaven and call it love. Know what it is? Evacuation. Now, me: once or twice a week, tops, that's it, I'm over the wall." She touched his mouth. "Why don't you smile, honey?"

It is told of the King of Tara's oldest son, the warrior prince, that, filled with ambition and lacking in sound Irish dread, he went out in a ghastly storm and dared the Scornful Witch of Fooley to show herself to him. Trees toppled at the very roar of thunder, even before the lightning struck; and people were tucked inside screaming prayers to the old gods and, just in case, to a few saints as well. But the warrior prince of Tara stood fast, and the Scornful Witch of Fooley showed herself to him, and he was not afraid; but she cast a spell on him that he must run to a fight wherever it might be, and run to the next, and the next after, till, his health squandered, he must err in his feints and fall. They tell this in sorrow, for though the warrior was not a grand prince, he had the hope of loyalty to Tara, if only Tara would let him in.

"You should smile, Johnny," said Nora, in the parlor sorting records at her Victrola when he returned. "You look so much finer when you do. What girl would love a dreary man?"

"Where's da?"

"That," she said, "is a question for philosophers to try. Will you be nice to me tonight?"

"Where's the others?"

"Asleep. It's late. But not for us, is it? Is it, Johnny?"

Johnny went into the boys' bedroom. Mike and Dennis lay at opposite sides of the bed. Each of the three had a drawer sacred to himself, all prowling prohibited, and in his drawer Johnny had placed his gun inside a heavy, hollowed-out Bible, bound in rope. He tore the fastenings off, put the gun in his coat, and left the room; while his back was turned, he saw, Dennis and Mike had rolled into each other's arms.

Johnny went out and Nora said nothing.

He walked down Third Avenue into the forties, cut west, then slowed up around Times Square, looking for an available man. He followed a thin drunk out of a bar on Seventh Avenue, south a few blocks, then into Thirty-seventh Street, and came up behind him fast and true, the gun eloquent in the small of his back, to say, "One word and you die."

It was Johnny's fifteenth birthday.

Soon came summer, and Johnny stalked and danced all over the city. He made the acquaintance of rough, hard women—unlike Dublin Johnny, who liked them sweet and pleading no. But like his da, he seldom came home; for two months he lived with a prostitute on Forty-seventh Street, far west almost to the river. She retired when Johnny began spending the night, knowing that once the sex flagged they'd begin to fight and after making up the sex would get even better—for a man is at his sharpest when comforting a woman he has hurt—and then it would flag again and the fights would get worse and the making up sluggish. And then he'd leave her and she'd be back on the street. Not a bad vacation for a working girl.

"Where'd you learn to do all that?" she asked him one night, just after. "A raw kid like you."

"My da is the King of Tara," said Johnny. "He lent me his charm."

"Oh, I should have guessed that right off." She had learned to restrain her laughter around him, learned the hard way, because he was quick to teach. But irony he allowed. Indeed, da had taken him aside one day and told Johnny how to get a woman to do anything you want: for what father with such power will not pass it on to his son? Johnny had gone right to Gilda Bono to try it, but she was smart and got back into the sunlight before he could make the first kiss and plant the magic. Then Johnny tried it on Carolyn Leera, known to the neighborhood as Saint Lie-down; but that proved nothing because, if the rumors were true, Johnny could have had her anyway. Finally he tried Margaret Cashlin, and he knew this to be a sound test because she wept so when he got hold of her, and seemed so frightened. She even fought him. Then he went through the steps, as Dublin Johnny had outlined them.

"On the eyes, first," Dublin Johnny had warned, "as they struggle, and keep at it till they weaken. It helps if they're a certain bit unlaced already then, for there's a lot in how you hold them. How you make them look up at you, to see a man. They need to see, Johnny. When you get to the between of the thighs, they'll be very sudden quiet, you know."

Johnny learned that it was true, for Margaret Cashlin seemed to see Johnny in quite a different way at that moment, and he paused

45

in his test and stroked her hair, and went back to kissing her. She had been planning to become a nun. And when she looked up at him again, she was weeping for joy.

The prostitute would not let Johnny keep his gun in her place; otherwise she gave in to him in all. He basked in that. Imagine, all you need do is take them to bed and they'll watch you as if you were a parade.

"I like you, Johnny," she would say, at the oddest times. He liked her back. But all the prostitutes in the world liking you cannot redeem a lack of resonance in your family dealings. Even a whispered revenge couldn't really help. One day da warned Johnny he was coming home that night, and Johnny contrived to get a live mouse into da's cigar box and blame it on Mike. But somehow Dennis got into it. And, after all was spent, the little boy hated Johnny more than ever, and had to be sent to live with Aunt Molleen.

There was another prostitute, and more after. Johnny found them uniquely appreciative. They liked to bathe him, tease him, praise him. A man grows up longing to please a woman, then, grown, learns to be pleased. They love a warrior, you know; they love a man. This is his inheritance: to become as his da, only more so and less, more the blundering taker and less the goodtime companion. And Johnny knows this. Oh, he knows it. No pubs for him, where the men hang out to regale each other with stories. Johnny is always in a secret and private place. The thief, not afraid to hurt someone. Because he has realized that by hurting you get what you need. People will not give anything up otherwise.

Now, there was in those days a certain athletic association called Steel Fist, which held bare-knuckles contests in one of the little old arenas on lower Second Avenue that had been abandoned when the gala New York town moved from Fourteenth Street way up into the forties and fifties. Once, sons of the Irish Calcutta known as Five Points tried their luck, stamina, and savagery on each other while sporting gentlemen looked on to place wagers on regular favorites or a promising tyro.

A Steel Fist encounter took on the outline of a boxing match in having a roped ring, timed rounds, and a referee, but otherwise went its own way. Any man who wished could play contestant, strip off his shirt, and fight another man. There were no rules. After a few minutes, one man stood and another was down. Then two other men faced off, and the two winners fought each other in the third match. So it went through an evening of hoarse shouts—"Fifty bucks on Big Red!"—and the occasional donnybrook among the spectators, heartened by the show, till one man had bested all challengers and won the prize bag of one hundred dollars cash. Steel Fist was against the law, but the police—being, as you might say, friends of the committee—looked on with fond tolerance. A few even entered the lists themselves.

"I wouldn't think of taking those other two along to here," said Dublin Johnny and he and Johnny settled in. "Babes in bibs."

The first match ended a draw, as both men collapsed more or less simultaneously, but the second found one so ahead of the other that the downed man, a lad of twenty-one or so, went into convulsions as he lay; and the winner, appearing again a bit later, was so taken by the effects of a deceptively skinny fellow with a fast boot that he staggered ten feet backward and vomited. Now, which would be more opportune in such a meeting, strength or will?

Johnny looked about the arena and nudged his da in the matter of a dingy-looking man who had brought along a colorful lady friend, one of the few women present. It was clear from their behavior that he took her to Steel Fist the way some men eat oysters, to prepare local orbits for the conjunction of Mars and Venus. When a man went down, the woman screamed, but softly, confidentially, and the man would put his arm around her waist then, and give her a little push. Johnny watched them perhaps more than he watched the brawling, and wondered if a man should like a woman who was roused to love by substitute, because of other men's, therefore a false, violence.

"Only your own violence matters," Johnny said.

Dublin Johnny agreed. "To get in the ring and smash a man

47

down! To keep fetching on him! Will you look at them there?"

Two fine young boys they were, pounding and stamping. They could easily have been friends. It was a true but boastful violence, wasted to give strangers a laugh.

"Kill him!" a bald, fat ogre shouted.

"Kill yourself!" Johnny told him. "Or step in the ring with me."

The man pretended he hadn't heard, so Johnny leaned over and pulled him near by his shirt. "I said, 'Shut your fucking ugly face!' " Johnny remarked, shoving the fat man ass over teakettle. When Johnny turned back to the ring, one of the fighters, losing grip, was hanging on the ropes, weeping through his blood as the other held him by the hair and punched his face till he sagged away.

It was Uncle Flaherty who got hold of Dublin Johnny to say that Nora was dead, and Dublin Johnny who told Johnny; and Dublin Johnny had no more to say than the mere fact of it and Johnny said nothing at all. He felt they had pushed him out of the family, and it was not his obligation now to feel bereft. He knew well that it was a poignant time, but why should he feel sentimental? Oh, and he would not weep at the wake for the crowd to see. Is that what they hope? "Maybe you'll kneel for her at the last," said Dublin Johnny, "and maybe you won't. It's your choice, Johnny. Watch those two mollycoddles ache at the coffin, though. They'll be on the floor sober, and so thorough it'll take Father Doyle the afternoon to scrape them off."

It was the night of Steel Fist, but Dublin Johnny thought it would be improper to attend the fights on the eve of his wife's wake. He'd best just go out and get plastered, show respect for the dead. But he did not move at first, and the two men were quiet for a bit. Dublin Johnny took Johnny by the shoulder—his only son in one way of viewing it—and looked hard at him, questioning hard.

Will you keep the secret? Are we together in it? Do you know why it is better to make love to women than to love a woman? Do you understand what power there is in love, what anger?

48

Young Johnny met his father's gaze, and dully nodded, and Dublin Johnny went away then. But Johnny still thought about these questions, and he became unnerved, and he stormed through the town with his gun, but he could not concentrate on his rounds. Well, Nora and all. So he went, on ice, to Steel Fist, signed up, and waited restlessly in the dressing room. It would not be disloyal to note at this point that many of the contestants are taller and heavier even than Johnny. But he has a particular gusto tonight. Nora is the referee for his first fight, and Dennis rings the mat in fifty faces, as Johnny pulls out the left feint-right smash and socks it true over and over till his opponent's knees bumble him down, and as Johnny goes to scoop him up for more, his opponent pleadingly spits out something Johnny can't hear, but is probably "We hate you," and Johnny finishes him off quickly.

Just before his second fight, Aunt Molleen runs into the ring to lodge a protest, but everyone ignores her, and his opponent whispers, "Can I come along with you?", so Johnny bashes him with both fists like pistons. Later, the man staggers in circles and as Johnny comes toward him he puts a hand out against Johnny's chest, gently, as if to ask out of the competition. But that would be contrary to the rules, so Johnny grabs that hand and swings him into the rope and kicks him down screaming.

In the dressing room, waiting for the third fight, Johnny looks around for Mike, his next opponent, and hopes that Dennis, all of him, is still in the audience. Between matches, Nora and Dennis would dance in the ring. Did you know they danced together? There are people who take hold and people who want to be held: the killers and the lovers. Dennis visits Johnny in the dressing room, and Johnny hugs him one last time, because after this they will not be friends again. Dennis whistles for Johnny, and tells him how he and Mark Revien followed old Mrs. Trentino into Gristede's and blew their noses in her dress and when she turned around they said, "Hey lady, can you direct us to the Kaopectate?" Nora is dancing and Johnny rocks Dennis. He tells him that he did hold him under the water at the beach, but not to drown him. He reminds Dennis that when he pulled him up out of the water and Dennis was coughing, he held onto Johnny as if he were the lifeguard. Johnny sets him down and Dennis backs away, so Johnny goes after him and Dennis runs into the ring shouting for Mike, but Johnny catches Mike and Nora tries to pull Johnny off. He keeps slamming Mike, and slamming him, and this feels so right and free that Johnny is howling with pleasure, and Mike is in the ropes now, blood all over his face, and Johnny is smashing at his head and the bell clangs and the referee tries to drag Johnny off but Johnny pulls Mike away from the ropes so he can kick his head and stomp him into pulp, smite him.

It took five men to drag Johnny off his opponent, a forty-year-old mechanic whose first and last Steel Fist this was, and Johnny was disqualified for Inconsiderate Brutality.

"Wasteful," Johnny murmured, when he got to his girl's place that night. One look at him and she knew better than to ask, "Where have you been?"

"Wasteful," he said again. "Wrong people."

"What wrong people, honey?"

Yes, he will keep the secret, of how Nora died. Yes, he and Dublin Johnny are together in it; that is why Johnny will keep the secret, their secret, something done. You'll see. And yes, Johnny will only make love, never *love*, because he can comprehend passion but not affection. Love, in this part of Tara, is anger.

"My ma is dead," Johnny told his girl, pouring himself a drink.

She said nothing, waiting for more. But what more is there to say than that?

When his da fell out of work, Johnny stood by him, not that he himself knew why. They would pal around and talk. And Johnny told his da some of the doings with his gun, and Dublin Johnny extends his fist as he would. The youngster to do all that! He thought it a fine joke, and said his boy was the Great American Johnny after all.

Johnny said that he had in mind certain professional expansions and needed a partner he could absolutely trust.

"I'm the one!" cries Dublin Johnny, yet more amazed at this absurdly gifted boy, a bold man in his teens. And Johnny is exact now in what he does and how he moves. Suddenly he is smiling. Because his smile scares fools, and there's a way to have what you want. Dublin Johnny, who has known that about a big man's smile all his life, at last feels close to his boy, Great American Johnny, the warrior prince, the smiter.

But the warrior prince, woe to Tara, was born to die in battle with a dragon.

The Story of
IRON MIKE

M ike got his nickname the day he repulsed an intrusion by the Gramercy Boys, come up to Turtle Bay to mooch around and insult the neighborhood. Ordinarily, local defense was the office of the Fifty-fifth Street Brigade, but Johnny's gang was nowhere about when Mike, then nine-and-a-half, saw a group of strange kids annoying Gilda Bono.

Maybe she was big enough to take care of herself—she had a good four years on Mike, anyway. But she started asking these guys' names and what school they went to, a patently nosy act in these parts, and saying she was going to tell Father Doyle, which did not impress the Gramercy Boys overly much. The biggest one —he might have been fourteen or so—said if that's the way she felt about it, maybe she ought to show them her finkie.

So Gilda hauls off and slaps him, and for maybe four seconds he was shocked, but at the fifth second he hit her back. By then Mike was already running over to take on the whole lot, if that's what he had to do. Luckily, Gilda had begun screaming by then, and neighborhood kids of all sizes began to pour out of the buildings, so Mike was alone in the fray for only a short while. At that, the appearance of several high-schoolers turned the battle into the massacre of the Gramercy Boys, who ran squealing home to ma. Gilda immediately proclaimed the greatness of Mike, saying he was the most gallant boy in the neighborhood, and she always knew he was; so the bigger boys took note of him, and said he was all right and they had had their eye on him for a good man long since.

So Mike was the hero, and who should come along then but the Father himself, and Gilda runs up to him and tells him how Mike saved the neighborhood somewhat single-handedly.

"That's an encouraging report," says Father Doyle. "But I'd take more joy of it to see your family in church this Sunday, Parnell Keogh."

"The man of iron," Gilda enthused, not to change the subject, but the Keoghs were naturally unchurchly and Father Doyle will go on sometimes.

"Iron Michael Keogh," said one of the guys, trying it out.

"Iron Mike," said another.

A chorus of yeahs. Iron Mike it will be.

And they all sauntered off to the Bon Ton Coffee Shop to treat Iron Mike to a deluxe. As they turned onto Second Avenue, there was Mike's brother Dennis and Mark Revien, hands in their pockets and whistling at each other in this code they had devised because Mike had taught Dennis to whistle and now it was as if Dennis couldn't do anything else. The two little boys stared in wonder at the parade, and Gilda, serving as official hostess, cried out, "Iron Mike is the most exciting boy in the neighborhood!", which did not explain a great deal but left Dennis with the feeling that his family had come into renown. As they swept by, Mike pulled Dennis along with them.

"Why does she call you Iron Mike?" Dennis asked.

"Hey, that's a long story, sport," Mike replied, unsure as to how embarrassed he ought to be, and knowing Dennis would soon have it in a hundred versions anyway.

"Iron Mike," said Dennis. "Jeepers."

54

"Sure," said Mike.

"Iron *Mike!*"

His mother called him Parnell, looking down with that wry smile that told you she wanted to share a secret or two and to hell with the trouble it would cause. "Parnell," she would say, as soft as a kiss when they were alone, crisp when his da was about. She was a no-nonsense mother. That suited Mike, for he liked things plain and fair. Some mothers were fancy or jokey, like Sneaky Pazillo's, yelling out of the window at everyone or singing at the dinner table —which, though it was disloyal to Sneaky to think so, was particularly irritating since all she ever made for dinner was sandwiches. Some mothers were too weak to do their job. Aunt Molleen, if she'd been a mother, would have been a flop, much as Mike loved her. There is such a thing as being too gentle; and she giggled and blushed like Gilda's sister Charlene.

No, Mike's ma was a true thing, running the guest house and seeing to the food—breakfast and dinner came with the bed—and raising three children and putting up with a disorderly husband. Sometimes Mike wondered what his granduncle Flaherty would have been like as their da, but it was unfair to dwell on such matters. Your family is your family—make the best of it.

You know, sharing a house with people can teach you things. How to get along with different sorts of people, for one thing. How to help the ones you like get closer to what dreams will inspire them, for another—and the opposite of that is: how to know when the ones you don't like won't ever be worth anything, so you'll have to fight them or get out of their way. Look at the cards Mike drew in the immediate family, for an illustration: a great ma and a worthless da, never around except to give her grief about how his sons are all a shabby rabble. Says it straight out, he does, too, with us there to hear. Well, one of them is rabble all right, that skunk Johnny. But Dennis is going to turn out fine. Not much good in a fight, maybe, but he's an arty kid, and they're not supposed to be fighters. He's funny when he dances with ma to the Victrola. It's a pretty sight, and it tells you something about a family right there, because she's helping him know about how a man should treat a lady, and he looks cute because he's so serious about it. Ma's very good about trying not to laugh. Dennis has sound values, too, like once you're in with him, you're in for life: which is the way a man should carry his relationships. Not like da, who keeps forgetting he has a family and then suddenly shows up, oh hello there where's my dinner? Or like Johnny, who's making all these overtures to you one minute and the next is lying in wait for you behind a door.

From the first, Uncle Flaherty kind of squired Mike around as his substitute da, and gave him politics, which is how to understand what your kind is meant to be in the world. "And who's in charge of that?" was Uncle Flaherty's answer to a great many questions: Who's responsible? Who takes the profits? Who'll do the labor? "Mike, my boy," he says, "no one's on your side but *your* side," and that's politics. "The whole rest of it is deals."

"Who's our side?" said Mike.

"Who else but the working Irish of the city of New York?"

"Well, who are the other sides, then?"

"Everybody else, of course. Where've you been, boy, that you don't see the variety of kind and purpose in the world? You're living in the most various town in the world as it is!"

"What's various about it?"

"I'll tell you, Mike. Various means the Police and the Fire belong to us, the schools belong to the Jews, construction belongs to the Italians, Poles, a few Indians from Canada, and the Irish who couldn't get into Police and Fire. Chinatown and its concessions belong to the Chinese. Cheap restaurants to the Greeks and some more Italians. The niggers get what's left. That's New York, Mike."

"No, it's not. What about politicians? And the rich?"

"The rich get the terraces and the taxis and whatever else they have in mind to have, including the politicians. Never get mixed up with the rich, Mike, not that the like of us would get the chance. It's a snake pit with a million snakes, all of them going after each other. Biting, swallowing snakes, Mike. That's why the city is

56

growing so. Before the war it was stable, everything sitting tidy where it was. Watch the doom coming now: in twenty years, it'll be changed into a garden of the rich."

"How come you like building so much, then? Aren't you working for them?"

"Ain't got a choice not to, lad. If you build, you build for the rich, for sure in damnfool no one'll ever get a chance to build for the poor. Be you the one, then, Mike. Go up with it, for there's a living in it, even power, to a point. It's a rough business. I'll say so. But which ain't? When it's time, I'll put you forth for your book the way I did your da. Only your family can get you into the union, you know. That way, we control what's ours. You'd fancy being an ironworker, wouldn't you, Mike?"

"Sure I would."

"Not forever, though. We're going to see what else you can do in running your own little end of things. Maybe sheet metal or cement. You're bright, Mike, and you've got stone in you. Not like your da—he's all fire. Maybe I'm sorrowful to tell his own son, and maybe I ain't. But it's so. When he first came over, I thought he had the stuff. But he can't concentrate on anything. He's always off and doing. And doing what?"

"What?"

"Never mind what. You're a good boy, Mike. Just remember to be kind to your ma and your Aunt Molleen. They're my brother's own children, and, after me, it's you who'll be taking care of them, I think."

"It's a little early, isn't it? To be telling me that?"

"Mike, you'd be surprised how fast it goes."

The most exciting boy in the neighborhood tends to have a good childhood, and Mike developed with few untoward incidents. There was a bad spill in their new apartment when da came home in a drunken ecstasy and tried to persecute Mike and Dennis. Ma fought the man with a terrible strength you'd not expect from a woman, but it was a mad scuffle all over the place, and finally da threw Dennis into the boys' bedroom and locked the door before

Mike and his ma could save him. Mike suffered torments for some time after that, for ever since the big holiday on the Jersey shore, Dennis and he had understood a kind of pact, and Mike had never let him down till then. Ma was troubled, too, and did not always carry herself with her accustomed pride after.

Mike believed in a Manichaean interpretation of The Theory of the Luck of the Irish. He felt instinctively that somehow the warring forces of the universe maintain their contentions in balance—so that for every blow for the bad guys the goods guys get one, though they may not recognize it as such. And the Irish get two. Perhaps this was why Mike was the last of his family to leave the Church, and did not leave it as much as agree not to trouble it further. He had seen his friends taking comfort, at a time of death, in the epic of an everlasting universe; heard the love that is fear of God soothing the war tales of his friends' fathers, forgiving them for their cruelty as, at the time, it must have urged them on to it.

It was hard to miss how the character of Mike's family responded exactly by type to the teachings and practices of Father Doyle, head of the parish. Da and Johnny had none of it; and that was their recklessness. Ma held it at a distance, but that was ma, forgivably suspicious of a rival sovereign. Aunt Molleen surrendered because it was her nature not to resist. Uncle Flaherty held firmly against it because he was an unromantic man, with no love for mysteries, a man of crafts and science. And of course Dennis thought of asking all those questions that you can't answer, like, "If it's a sin to beat off, how come you're always doing it?"

In some ways, Dennis was like Mike's little boy, admiring him unconditionally and always trying to find out something a man needs to know. Mike felt good if he could tell him. Like when Mike whistled at something cute and Dennis would ask why she looked annoyed and Mike could explain that girls did that to pretend they didn't want to know who you were. A guy feels outstanding to know that, once he gets old enough, he can talk right up to them, tell them who he is and ask how they're feeling, and maybe take them for a deluxe or even dancing.

58

Probably Dennis was right to question the Church's rules about sex—it showed a sensible nature, didn't it? Uncle Flaherty said as much, when Mike asked him how he should handle it. "It's good that you're letting him come to you," his uncle added, "so he'll not pick up foolish stories from his friends and hatreds from the Catholic eunuchs. I've seen what happens when men grow up fearful of their own bodies, and the stuff inside them. Desire may not be as worthy as love but it's as human a failing. Men that can't see that, half the time they got to act as if they've no cock on them at all. Every sensitive thing in them has to be a secret. A lie. I'll tell you—it's a mark of what kind of man you are, how far you've allowed yourself to travel on that road of denial and hellfire and prevaricating Father Doyles. Or have you already been informed as to the style of tea he takes with the Widow Briley?"

Mike had heard.

"See, Mike, the smart ones don't let the Church get too deeply into them because all the evidence of their feelings tells them how daft the Church is on every subject but prayer and death. The smart ones keep their counsel, see what I mean? It's the jerks who bow down to it all, and mix themselves up, and say such stupid things that no sound man'll respect them ever after. That's why I like to hear you speak freely on it to me, and help Dennis too. Maybe it runs in the blood—God knows your da has no trouble accommodating his appetites, and he's as Catholic as any by birth and education. Now, watch out for Dennis like a good brother, and make sure he comes out a smart one."

Mike guessed he was a good brother, then, for he not only watched out for Dennis but made sure he threw out a word to him when Mike was out with his friends and Dennis and Mark Revien would come scooting around a corner, or when Mike would pass them, sitting on Mark's stoop making up dumb songs. Virtually all Mike's friends had brothers and sisters, but you'd think they were all strangers the way they ignored each other in public. Gilda Bono would appear not to know her own kid sister; and when Sneaky Pazillo's older brother Pat worked one summer behind the counter at Coffey's, he made Sneaky promise not to enter the store on pain of instant and total death. True, Mike and Johnny didn't trade a word. But that was different. Dennis said that when he saw Johnny he would run away. Now they saw Johnny as seldom as they saw da.

The rest of the family was intact; certainly the neighborhood had plenty that weren't. Girls married too young; boys got into trouble and went to jail. Somehow Mike found himself at the center of his clan, proudly holding them together, for though he kept quarters in his ma's apartment, he spent many an evening with Dennis at Aunt Molleen's, and had dinner out with Uncle Flaherty once a week. Sometimes he stayed over at Aunt Molleen's, telling himself he was cherishing his kind; but perhaps he was escaping his ma's quirks, which had been growing more opulent every year. He could not concentrate on his schoolwork, or the construction studies Uncle Flaherty set him, with blueprints and cost estimate sheets, for she would be on him, or staring at him in a wild hat, and when he'd look up she'd put her index finger to her lips and wink at him. Or the Victrola would be going.

"Ma, why don't you get out more?" he kept asking. "You're always in."

"I am where I live."

He tried another tack: "Aunt Molleen could use a night out. Why don't you take her to a movie?"

"Oh, Molleen doesn't approve of me. Never did. She gets all so poignant about it, now. I'd rather dream. I'll dream of you, Parnell."

When he found her, lying on the ground floor of the building, at the center of the stairwell, her neck broken and her soul gone to peace, he thought, all at once, that she had slipped on the stairs, and that she was joking, and that a criminal was loose in the neighborhood, and that this was her dream. He stayed calm, but his voice shook as he spoke to her, kneeling there, and he was afraid to touch her, move her, hurt her, but he must hold her in case she was cold. The body was warm, as shattered as the emerald necklaces the Scornful Witch of Fooley would grind into her pastry

60

flour; and Mike, realizing that she must have fallen from a height, looked up through the stairwell as if trying to understand how she might have felt when it happened, how it looked to her, worrying that she might not have fallen, but jumped—yet why would she have done that unless they hadn't loved her enough? It was only Dublin Johnny Keogh who didn't, and Mike spoke to her in case she wasn't dead and was wondering if he loved her. He worried about calling an ambulance but he would not leave his mother alone. It was up to him to protect her.

The ambulance and the police did come, so he must have called them; he thought he did; it seemed he had. But it was Mrs. Deeny who buzzed them in, and she said she had called them, because she was going out to the market and perhaps see about some cigarettes, her only vice if you must know, and she saw the boy on the floor with Nora Keogh. And when Mrs. Deeny asked him what happened, he looked at her as if he couldn't see her. So she told them. Mike was in no state to contradict her, and the police treated him gently, but they wouldn't let him ride in the ambulance, because the medic said Nora Keogh was quite extremely dead from a fall of considerable reach. Mrs. Deeny said she'd better take Mike to Molleen Flaherty's, the unmarried sister of the late Nora Keogh, and nearly a foster mother of the two youngest boys. The police wanted to drive her and Mike, thinking he was already a very good choice for a suspect, but Mrs. Deeny refused to ride with them out of fear that her enemies would be glad to make a blameful construction of spotting her in a police car. It was only a few blocks, and they walked.

On the way, Mrs. Deeny narrated a bit of the Keogh family history, and then the police decided they ought to make the acquaintance of Dublin Johnny. On the way down Second Avenue, Mrs. Deeny signalled to a few pets of hers that something big was on the way, and a minor parade built up at a respectful distance behind them, Mrs. Deeny patting Mike's shoulder between the two policemen and her enemies, she was certain, cowering in their rooms to see her in civil glory.

As they reached the corner of Fiftieth Street, Dennis and Mark

Revien came whirling by and began to whistle, but Mike went up to Dennis and Dennis saw his face and stood very still, and Mike whispered to Dennis as Mrs. Deeny identified him. Mike was crying now, Dennis not, but Mike held his hand anyway. As Mrs. Deeny remarked to her friends behind them, "Isn't it the end of childhood for the Keogh brothers now?"

The end of high school, at any rate, marked Mike's entrance into the building trade, as he and Uncle Flaherty had been planning it since ever. There was no doubt for them that Mike would become an ironworker, for there, Uncle Flaherty alleged, lay the core of it all. A lazy man may herd with the electricians or carpenters; and a smart man will eventually start his own firm. But first he must learn, and see how the world is built. And this is the task of the ironworker.

"They're a rough lot," Uncle Flaherty warned him, for they obey no rules but their own. "Take everything they say in fun, no matter how it sounds to you," for they are a blunt people. "Give them time to read you, and to like you, for they will, Mike. Everyone likes you, lad." And once they like you, you have their loyalty for life.

Mike was the punk, in their terminology, and at first had little more to do than fetch the coffee, cart matter about, relay messages from one end of the site to the other, and, occasionally, when least expecting it, catch a thrown wrench when someone casually called out, "Jump, you fucker." He was attentive, watching how everything fit together, asking some of the other jobbers about their trades; and he did not miss the spirit of the damned hero that infused all that the ironworker said and did. The other unions bore somewhat civilized men to the site—husbands and fathers, holders of mortgages, sports fans. But the ironworkers were untamed, men who had carved themselves of stubborn stone, fearless and dangerous. This was Dublin Johnny's union, after all, the adventurous element. The other unions crept onto the site after the frame had begun to rise, sheltered on flooring and behind safety fences and coddled in temporary elevators: it was the ironworkers who climbed into the air and pulled the pieces of a new building up after them. The crew comprised setters and bolters, the first to fit the girders together and the second to fasten them. All ironworkers could handle both jobs, but most favored one or the other, and Mike asked Uncle Flaherty which he ought to be.

"It's your choice, lad," said Uncle Flaherty. "You make it."

Uncle Flaherty had not specialized in his youth, being handy at anything, and now, because of his age, he was a foreman. Still, he had not let liquor and heeling around make a ruin of him, as some did—as Mike's da had done. Uncle Flaherty stood straight and sturdy yet, with the strenuous, thick-set shoulders and heavy walk the work put on a man, and, the day they set up the derrick, he climbed the central tower, hand over hand, forty-five feet straight on, and no one thought anything of it but Mike.

Ironworkers collaborated in two-man teams, and Uncle Flaherty warned Mike to choose his partner carefully: an unreliable mate could get a man injured, even killed. In the event, Mike's partner chose him—Pete Reever, nicknamed, perhaps ironically, the Duke. Ironworkers were generally sizeable, but Pete was a monster: and the most aggressive of the gang in lunch-break courtship. While the other unions wandered off to various favorite eating places on staggered hours, the ironworkers held court from noon to half-past, sitting in single file against a wall across the street from the site. There they romanced the women who passed, all women, from startled schoolgirls to rigid ladies of fashion. It was a questionable sport, without shape, and never a goal scored, for few women took notice of the ironworkers' summaries and entreaties, and those who did reacted with either a dear hurt or a most uncomely rage. What kind of man would delight to inspire either? Mike wondered, sitting with his comrades in the line and trying, and failing, to laugh along with the rest. Pete the Duke was always at the heart of the noontime action, standing lone and feral at the edge of the sidewalk to pull deep breaths into his shirtless chest as a pretty woman went by—"delicacy," he called them, and his eyes shone, but his mouth seemed to sneer.

Pete helped Mike over some of the tricky parts of his apprenticeship, advising him as to who could be counted on and who was, as Pete put it, "wreckage." And he did, unquestioningly, throw his weight behind Mike, speeding Mike's acceptance by the confraternity. At the bull sessions after work in the shabby midtown taverns that the great world scarcely notes and never enters, Pete would sit close to Mike, warning him with a touch of his thigh when Mike was treading hazardous ground and must retreat or risk an explosion. Though Mike had joined the setting crew, guiding the bones of a new office building into their sockets alongside Pete the Duke, Mike was technically still a punk, a bozo kid who'd best second his seniors' opinions or keep his to himself. Once, after Mike had shared Uncle Flaherty's social breakdown of the professions of New York City, an ironworker named Bouncer Joe said, mildly, "That can be. That can be, no doubt. But I truly do fear I am detecting a Communist viewpoint of some kind as I sit here. You a Communist, punk?"

Mike, confused, willing to be identified neither as a Communist nor as this man's flatterer, was considering uttering a "Hell, no," when Bouncer Joe turned to Danny Fisheater and said, "Sounded plain Commie pinko to me. How'd it sound to you?"

Before Danny Fisheater could answer, Pete the Duke, also mildly, said, "It sounds to me like this: anyone rides the punk going to ride me first. Have to."

Now, Bouncer Joe is two hundred twenty pounds in flesh and a steamroller in mentality, but Pete the Duke is the size of a small brownstone. Bouncer Joe shrugs, meaning it is okay with him, and that is that.

After the others had gone, Mike thanked Pete for standing up for him.

"Sure," said Pete, signalling the bartender for another round.

"I hope I can do the same someday," said Mike, embarrassed by his own words.

"You won't have to," Pete told him. True enough.

"Well, I . . . I can take care of myself, anyway."

Pete nodded. "Sure you can, baby."

"So why'd you do it?"

"So what, though?" Pete looked at him. "That bozo is wreckage. Come on, he's bozo."

"But why?"

"Because I'm soft on you," Pete said, and laughed, and hit Mike's arm so hard it ached for two days.

"Why do you have to know him?" Dennis fussed at Mike. "Your other friends aren't like that!"

"It takes all kinds, sport. Anyway, this is a different world, building. You can't expect everyone to be like Sneaky Pazillo or Mark Revien."

"He plays too rough. When he thinks he's being friendly to me he's bending my arm behind my back, or he holds my head so I —"

"He's just playing with you, little brother. That's how ironworkers play."

"You don't play like that."

"Yeah, that's because . . . because I know you. I know you wouldn't like it. I'm careful with you because that's how brothers should be."

"Do you play rough with Pete?"

"Sure." Sure. "It's just a way of . . . for fun. For solidarity."

"Politics?" said Dennis.

"Sort of."

"How come whenever I see two guys who are friends, one is good-looking and the other isn't?"

That gave Mike pause. "Huh?"

"Like you and Pete. Because you're handsome and Pete's kind of—"

"That's only because you're my—"

"Well, he is. And it's always someone handsome with someone not. And I've watched them when they're looking at girls. And the handsome one—"

"Coincidences."

65

"No, it's—"

"Guys don't care about things like that. When you're friends it's because—"

"I always see it, Iron Mike. It's like the good-looking guy doesn't want anyone around to take away from his attention, and the bad-looking guy wants to borrow—"

"No, when guys are buddies—"

"Then why are you—"

"You're wrong, because that's not the way—"

"What about—"

"Because it's *not*. It's not, little brother. And it's not." He patted Dennis' shoulder; there are some things Mike will not hear.

"Okay, Iron Mike," says Dennis.

"Hey, come on, how are you getting on with your school work?"

"You'd look different," says Pete the Duke, "if you had money."

"Sure as hell," says Mike. "I'd wear a tie and stuff. One of those neat coats like on TV. Two pairs of pants."

"No, no, no," says Pete, slurring it out forcefully. Shakes his head. Turns his can of beer on the table. No. Looks at Mike.

Why are we friends? Mike thinks. I never know how to deal with this guy. "So what?" Mike says. "Huh?"

"I don't mean you'd dress different, baby. I mean you'd look different. People with money, they don't fucking look like us."

"Well, they shave for one thing, you crazy slob."

"I don't mean that, even. Maybe that's part of it." More circles of beer. Testing the wetness on the table with his finger. "Maybe. Fuck. Because what it is, they stand different, they move different, they smile different . . . their fucking eyes is different. Their eyes."

"Hell—"

"You look at a girl, Mike. You look at her, like right now, out on the boulevard there. What does she see? She sees some guy wants to put his donkey in her cute little come hole. That's what she's thinking, buddy. Maybe slap her around a little, she don't give in easy. Which she won't. She sees it in your eyes."

"What about your eyes?" says Mike, not liking this.

66

"Hey, good buddy." Hand on his neck, tickles him. "I'm right there with you, ain't I?"

"So?" Shrugging him off.

"These lawyers and doctors and such. They was all at some shitcream university together, you know? Where they learn how to look at a girl so she don't feel the next thing is going to be rape. She looks at them, she sees like, Oh, let's have a cup of soda pop, honey. Or May I call you up for a game of chess and the reading of poems?"

"You think that's all they do?"

Pete shrugged. "They fuck sooner or later. That's all anybody does. But the point is, you get closer to them by looking as if *you don't want to!* Huh?"

They were heading for the site, to stand around—as ironworkers invariably do—till the very stroke of half-past, when lunch is over. On the way, several women passed, the prettiest of them, a sophisticated-looking young blonde with a bracing smile and smart clothes, treated to one of Pete's famous visual rapes, black eyes slitting her clothes from bodice to thigh, a deep, slow thrust of the hips, and a gaseous whisper of "Honey, my donkey knows that you are *good!*"

Whereupon the blonde stopped as if thinking of something, turned, and came back to Pete and Mike. "I just want to ask you," she told Pete, "what kind of man it takes to do that to a woman who has never harmed him in any way." She didn't gulp, or stutter, or bite the words off, as the few women who dared confront Pete did. She simply stated them. "What kind of man does it take, really?"

"It takes me," said Pete, pleased.

"It takes you," she said. She seemed to have run out of words, because after a few moments she turned to go. No, back she then came—charged, really. "Don't you have feelings? Don't you have a conscience?"

"How about a date?" said Pete.

"Don't you have a mother? How would you like a great beast like you to humiliate her in public?"

67

"I'd bust him dead." Pete flexed his biceps. "Feel that."

She turned to Mike. "Why don't you tell your foreman you're quitting for the day, you've already made your quota in insulting defenseless women?"

"Come on, lady," said Pete, looming over her. She stood her ground, her jaw so set it might have been last week's concrete. "If I had a monocle and a faggot bag," Pete went on, "you'd be arranging to meet me at the ballet, huh? A little *Dying Swan*, please, right? Or maybe my personal favorite, *The Sleeping Fruity?*"

"What on earth," she asked, "is a faggot bag?"

"He means a briefcase," said Mike.

"If you'll pardon me for saying so," she told him, "a hundred briefcases wouldn't get your friend into burlesque."

"See what I'm telling you?" said Pete to Mike. "It's not the clothes, it's how you look."

The blonde had turned and left without another word. Mike was looking after her. Pete was about to say something, but an intentness in Mike's eyes led him to hold silent.

Mike looked at Pete and looked back. Men of any other culture, any other class, any other union, would have settled it with some words bandied on the matter—perhaps an apology from Pete for shaming Mike in front of a woman he didn't even know. But ironworkers do not trade in niceties. And there was this: if she hadn't turned to confront Pete in his assault, neither man would have thought twice about it. It would have remained a secret act, connived at by Pete the Duke and all the women who walked by him in that existentialism of the Manhattan streets: if I don't regard you, you don't exist. This woman, however, broke the secret open and made Mike feel like a bad guy, the one thing he could not bear to be.

So, as Pete looked on, not approving, Mike ran after the woman. When he reached her, she was weeping—much as did the Princess Ebhandre when told of the disappearance of the fairy hedgehogs from the park of her castle: weeping upon the passing of something sweet from the world. Perhaps the blond woman was mourning the scarcity of gentle natures, the collapse of the social contract. At the sight of Mike, the blond woman moved faster, but he said, "Please," and touched her arm, and she stopped, not looking at him.

"I'm sorry," said Mike. "It's just . . . a joke he does. He doesn't mean to . . . make you. . . . "

"Of course he does. Cry." She fumbled in her purse for a handkerchief. "That's exactly what he means. He's telling me that no matter now nicely I'm dressed or how confidently I remember to walk, I'm still just a piece of—"

"Come on." Mike was wiping her eyes with his bandana. "Come on. That's not what he wanted at all."

"They're starting them in young nowadays. How old are you, sixteen?"

"Look, we're both sorry. Nineteen."

"I generally come this way on my lunch hour, so if I pass you again, please—"

"Wave at you. I'd be glad to." He smiled. "Come on. And you're not much older than me, so who are you to talk?"

"It's just so—"

"How old are you, anyway?"

"Don't you people ever give up?"

"Twenty-two?"

She started walking again.

"Twenty-three?" Mike considered running after her, stayed put, just nearly moving, stopping.

She kept going; when she turned the corner, Mike came back to Pete. They were late, but Pete had waited: loyalty among ironworkers is absolute. He said nothing to Mike, and his face showed nothing, but later that afternoon on the coffee break he said, "You apologize to that girl for me?"

"She was crying."

Pete nodded. "Don't do that again, baby."

"She was *crying*, Pete." Twenty-four at the most.

Pete looked like he was going to take a swing, but he suddenly picked up a stray tool, hefted it amiably, put it down. "Sure," he growled. "But don't."

"Anyway, she got my bandana."

That night, Pete called Mike at Aunt Molleen's to say he shouldn't have been so angry, come on over and we'll pop a few and like, maybe, who knows. Talk. Something. Pete lived a few blocks away in one of those renovated yet debased brownstones that were becoming common in the neighborhood, all the floor-throughs quartered into studios, unpainted, with the kitchen appliances set along one wall and the bathroom a cubicle in the corner. In the early 1970s, when the building trade was finishing off Sixth Avenue and just starting in on Third, such places were ideal for the vagabond ironworker, cheap, convenient, and as easy to acquire as to abandon. Landlords would not rent them to blacks and nobody else was interested. Little more than a decade later, people would vie for these regrettable closets with the money and nerve that New York never runs out of; for now, they were the province of semi-bourgeois crazies, degenerates, neighborhood veterans, and men like Pete.

Well, maybe he's kind of rough, Mike thought as he climbed the stairs to Pete's room, but he's a sound man. A solid buddy. Anyway, ironworkers are rough. It's a rough world, Mike's world, and even when I'm running my own firm and telling guys like Pete what to do, it'll still be rough. You don't get anywhere making love to strangers.

Pete, well along in his beer, gave Mike a big smile and clamped a headlock on him and dragged him all over the room to show him what a good mood he was in. Then he dumped him on the mattress, a bed of such disorder it was not merely on the floor but strewn over it. There was no place to sit in Pete's room except on the floor, which was just as well because the kind of couch a man like Pete would have had would probably be unsanitary, as stained with the blood of victims as the Druids' altar at Faincochbar, where, on windy nights, the echo of the screams of the chosen howls up and then swirls down the hills into the towns that love less importunate gods than the Old Ones were.

70

Mike sat next to Pete, their backs against the cracked plaster, their legs stretched before them, each set cradling a beer.

"Jo-Jo's coming over," said Pete. "You remember her?"

Mike vividly recalled the middle-aged adolescent who hung on the shoulders of ironworkers at lunch. They passed her from hand to hand nightly like a can of nuts you don't even bother to pour into a bowl. Somewhere, in some neighborhood, Mike was sure, a mother and father spent a section of each day trying to understand what damnhell mistake turned a sweet little kid into Jo-Jo.

"Soon as I hear the buzzer, old buddy," Mike began, but Pete cut in with "Fuck that, man. Jo-Jo likes *company.*"

"Well . . . "

"Hey. *Buddy.* Look alive and get set. What's mine is yours, right?" Punching his arm. "She's no delicacy, but she's okay."

Mike shook his head, trying to grin. "It's a crazy world for Jo-Jo, isn't it?" A rough world.

"Man, you are . . . she's getting what she wants, ain't she? It's not as if anybody's forcing her, or what?"

"It's hard to imagine Jo-Jo getting forced. That'd be like . . . like . . . "

"Like a french fry saying Don't eat me. Right?" Pete laughed; Mike didn't. "Right?"

"Yeah."

Pete looked Mike over. "Cool out, baby. It's a crazy world for everyone."

Jo-Jo clearly did not think so; she lit up like a holiday window display when she saw Mike. "Oh, I've always wanted him," she uttered.

"Everybody wants him, the fucker," said Pete.

Mike, embarrassed by the publicity, tried to shake it off in a strut.

"The fucker," Pete emphasized, lighting up a joint. Suddenly, no one said anything, and they smooched in silence, milling around in the room like spirits. Mike reminded himself that you retain your cool only when you don't have to remind yourself to retain it. When Jo-Jo pulled off her blouse Mike dutifully admired

71

her, and when she immediately turned to him and opened his pants, her eyes sparking into his, he smiled back. Nodded. Sure. Kissed her.

"Not like that," she told him. "Give it to me, boy. Tongue my soul."

Next thing Mike saw was Pete, nude, holding a tube of something. "Let's do it," he said.

"Both ways," said Jo-Jo, shuddering in a tiny riot as she reached for the tube.

"Let me," said Pete, taking hold of her so he could loosen her up. He glanced at Mike. "Get naked, kiddo. Curtain going up." He concentrated on Jo-Jo. "How's that feel, huh? Smooth and soothing, don't it, huh?"

She purred.

"Sure, lady. Relaxing with your friends. Nice night. Happy talk. Coming loose now, though. Just the way you want to be. Real honeybunch, now. Smooth, lady, sure."

She held Mike as if Pete weren't there, kissed him, frolicked as he entered her.

"Smooth," Pete urged, bending them back. "Smooth is ace tonight," so he could take her from behind.

Mike found it awkward trying to accommodate Jo-Jo's response to the rhythm of Pete's hips. They were silent again, till someone stumbled past Pete's door humming and Jo-Jo let out a batch of laughter. Then Pete grabbed Mike at the waist and built the tempo; and Mike, staring into Pete's eyes over Jo-Jo's shoulder, felt as if Pete were crashing through Jo-Jo to reach Mike. He pressed his mouth to Jo-Jo's, caught her hair, hoped to exult. And the silky feeling of her skin, the fast breathing, the tumult of the scandal! But, once it was over, he got out of there damn fast.

Dennis, in Aunt Molleen's front room, was dozing on the couch, his lap full of the notebooks in which he wrote his little songs. Mike sat next to him and watched Dennis' eyes open. Mike held out his arms and Dennis bumbled inside, pushing the picture of

72

Jo-Jo and Pete a bit to the rear. The pen Dennis always wore behind his ear tickled Mike's forehead.

"You never talk about ma, you know?" said Mike.

Dennis sleepily nodded, putting his papers into order.

"Why not?"

"I'm letting you mourn her for both of us."

Mike looked angry.

"What do you want me to do, light a candle?"

"Don't you talk that way!"

"Don't tell me what to do!"

Mike glared at him, sizing it up. Dennis looked away and worried. The fight dissolved.

"You be good or else," said Mike. "Okay?" His apology.

"Yeah."

"Okay."

"Forget it."

Mike smiled. "Class of '69."

"Two more months."

"What are you going to do, sport? Fixing to be an ironworker, maybe?"

Dennis smiled now. "I'm not like you, Iron Mike."

"Come on, little brother, you're just like me."

"We're all different, haven't you noticed that? Johnny. You. Me."

"*He* sure is."

Dennis had an odd look just then.

"What?" said Mike.

"Nothing."

"*What?*"

"I was . . . thinking of Nora."

"Good boy. Only don't call her that." Pete and Jo-Jo slid a bit further to the edge of Mike's vision as he checked the fridge for a snack. "Want an apple?"

"Iron Mike, if I have . . . like, a secret to tell you—"

"Don't." He flipped an apple at Dennis. "I don't like secrets. I don't want to keep them and I don't want to hear them. Okay?"

73

Dennis set his papers atop the piano and clipped the ear pen to his notebook.

"Okay, little brother?" That disappointed look on his face again, and he gets so quiet; but he's got to learn, and if Mike doesn't teach him, no one will. Mike compels himself to be hard, or the lesson won't take. Iron Mike, the most excellent boy in the neighborhood. "Answer me," he insists.

Dennis nodded, looking at the piano, and they sat, eating their apples. The loudness of the lack of conversation overwhelmed the crunching of the fruit. Finally Mike said, "We all have secrets, little brother." He himself had picked up a new one just a bit before. A real neat secret that Mike would bind up and store away and never share, no matter who. "And the reason they're secrets is they're too . . . too crazy to let out. People aren't supposed to know everything about you. They may not like you if they did. That's what secrets are for—to hide the rugged things so you can get along with people better."

"But why do *we* have to hide things? From each other? There's nothing you could tell me that would make me . . . not like you."

Mike imagined trying to tell Dennis what had just happened at Pete's, about the look in Pete's eyes and how trapped Mike had felt. "Don't be too sure of that, little brother. There are some amazing things going on."

"There were always amazing things. Uncle Flaherty says the first King of Tara had fifty wives."

"I mean more amazing than that." Still the hurt eyes. If the youngest brother is the least strong, is the oldest the strongest? "Fifty wives, huh? Sounds like a good deal."

Dennis didn't laugh.

"Okay, little brother. Maybe . . . if you really have to tell a secret, you can—but you better think about it real heavy first, because once it's out, it's trouble, and you can't push it back. I guess everyone has one secret he could maybe tell someone he trusts."

"One secret? I'm made of them."

*   *   *

74

It took six days, but Mike finally saw the blond woman again. She walked a little faster, pretending she hadn't spotted him, but he got right up to her and asked for his bandana.

"Unless you want to keep it," he added, staying with her. "You know, as a souvenir of Iron Mike Keogh."

She stopped abruptly, turned to him, opened her mouth, but had no sound in her. Not a word. Uh-oh, he had shocked her. Still, Mike had learned, women will more readily forgive you for asking for too much than for too little.

"You're right," he said. "I'm wrong. Of course you'll want to return it. We could have dinner and you—"

"If I told my big brother about this, do you know what he'd do?"

"He'd say, 'Give the guy his bandana back.'"

"No, he'd hand your head to you."

"I don't know. Embezzling a bandana without authorization . . ."

She laughed.

"See?" he said.

She shook her head. "How can you be so daring? What do you get?"

"Dinner with a pretty girl?"

This is what Mike saw in her face: she would like to meet him, but cannot accept an invitation from a stranger on the street.

Mike thought fast. "If we met at a party, wouldn't you say yes?" No, wait. "I mean, wouldn't you feel free to consider it?"

"Well . . ."

But, see, these parties they go to are their way of screening out the Wrong Element. That's why Mike couldn't get into them even if he knew where they were given.

"A friend with a wild sense of humor brought me, see?" he went on. "How I got there? And I'd be dressed up." At the moment, he's in an oversized white T-shirt and jeans the color of antique mud. "Come on, I'm a right guy."

He has said this just smoothly enough, as if he really believes it patent.

"Why me?" she asks.

"Because I feel guilty."

"About . . . that . . . "

"About . . . last week."

She squares her shoulders. "You're not the guilty party." Starting off again.

"Wait."

Hell, she does wait!

"I just know that I like you," he says.

"Do you realize that there's a four-year difference in our ages?"

"Twenty-three! I knew it! My favorite age! Anyway, in ten years, we'll be twenty-nine and thirty-three—the same generation!"

She laughed again.

"I bet your brother'd like me, too. Approve of me."

"I made him up."

"Defenseless, huh?"

Now one of those pauses. Searching looks, hands at the sides. Finally she says, "You're Italian, aren't you?"

"Irish."

"I'm sorry. I'm only allowed to date Jewish men."

This is so startling that she springs six feet out before Mike moves after her. "Who don't . . . allow you? At your age?"

"*I* don't. I'm sorry." She stops. "But really." What an attractive look of helpless sympathy to let a guy down with.

However, Iron Mike is standing on land mere inches from the place he grew up in, and draws therefrom a unique wisdom and an irresistible energy. "Okay, no dinner," he agrees. "But would you just come by here some more like this, on lunch? Just to talk?"

She smiles. "You're still nineteen, you know," she says.

"Twenty in November." Then he thinks, she had used the word *woman*—"what kind of man it takes to do that to a woman." That means she shakes hands with men. He extends his and she takes it.

"Mike," he says.

"Erica."

Wouldn't you know she'd have a hundred dollar name?

Mike is strong and pleasant, so of course she came back. True, he's too young: but he seems mature for a teenager, earnest, even—it's strange to say—fatherly. True again, he's not Jewish: but is it not time to dispense with that mystically defensive prejudice? From infancy, Erica had been warned that husbands who weren't Jewish drank, caroused, and beat their wives. She'd be miserable if she married out of the patriarchy, and her husband would throw her into the gutter, and don't come crying to us then! But Erica's mother had been born Christian; and while you can convert them, you can't ever deracinate them, not ever quite. Now and again Erica would sidle over to her mother when no one was listening and ask what it was about Christian men. And Erica's mother would tell her.

All Mike had to do was keep batting; she'd catch soon. The world of courtship is based on repetition, anyway. And, seeing that she held the neighborhood against him—a tough way of saying that she recognized a cultural antagonism—he attacked at the very center of her resistance by inviting her to an after-work tea at Aunt Molleen's. You can't judge a neighborhood by its streets; you judge it by its household sociability. Didn't ma used to say that? "Household sociability"?

"Just tea?" asked Dennis, as Mike checked him for neatness. "What kind of date is that?"

"It's where you don't have time for lunch and don't think you can land her for dinner yet."

"Mary and Joseph," said Aunt Molleen, coming into the bedroom. "There's something ruthless in the fruitbowl."

"It's a mango," said Dennis, whose job it had been to purchase the fruit. Mike was tying Dennis' tie for him. "I can do that myself," said Dennis. "I'm not a baby anymore."

No he wasn't, anymore. At an age, they pass from being held into people who hold. Good, Mike thought sadly. We're all men now. "Your knot is lopsided," he said, though, perking it up a bit.

Dennis covered the knot with his hand. "I tie it better than you do."

The buzzer rang.

"It's a what?" asked Aunt Molleen, picking at it.

"A mango."

Now, it is surely as plain as trees on a nearby hill that a sweet shamrock of Molleen Flaherty's class, raised in churchly obedience, will
not bloom as liberal-headed as we might wish for our heroines. Lo,
what are we mortals? Clay. So it was that, when Mike told Molleen
that Erica's last name was Van Duyck, she hid a touch of resentment
that a fine, friendly Irish boy like Parnell Michael is going off among
the Dutch gentry. Then she realized that this meant the girl must be
a spawn of Protestants, and took out her resentment to show it to the
world, and to Mike. But when he innocently added that there was
the feeling somewhere about in it that Erica Van Duyck was Jewish,
Aunt Molleen responded with a pestering fling of observations on
intermarriage, especially intermarriage with children, and not omitting intermarriage with children when the mother is Jewish. So offi-
cious and unfeeling was the scope of her assault that I hesitate to set
it before my readers, for fear of offending their sensitivities with the
bitter flavor of the earth's clay.

Nor shall I dwell upon the tea, with its precarious moments of
faux pas and sudden hush, except to note that Dennis kept things
moving nicely as the most sophisticated of the Keoghs: not worldly
but at least aware of what worldliness might be. The party gave
out after an hour, for Mike had determined to move carefully with
his young lady, and not to overburden her with the ways of his
peculiar people.

The first thing she said when he took her downstairs to walk her
to her taxi was, "You don't look a thing like them, you know."

The first thing Aunt Molleen said was, "I never felt so Irish in
my life. Where does a New York girl learn to talk like that? And
how old do you guess she is, esh? She's thirty if she's more than
eight!"

"She knew what a mango was," said Dennis.

"What was it about the Prince of Tara and the lovely foreign
princess? Did your da ever tell you boys of it?"

"If it's Tara, he told us a hundred times."

"And you never listening. There were three princes in it. And one of them married a stranger."

"Lots of people end up married to strangers," said Dennis. "For life."

"But this one started so . . . will you hark at the boyo! Who would you mean, for life?"

Dennis shrugged. "She's lovely anyway, isn't she?"

"Ah, you'd be sure of Mike to choose pretty ones. He has the way with him, like your da."

They grew silent, sitting at the table, Mike gone—actually a great many gone, and these two left, thinking of how The Way drove Dublin Johnny into a thousand beds, plying the charm that ruined him, and ruined Nora, and others. But Mike has no charm, these two know: Mike is just Mike.

"It was the mason prince, I think," Aunt Molleen finally said. "The one who married the princess. And there's a witch in it, too, now. And she asks the mason to build a tower so high no one ever sees the top of it through the clouds."

"And she imprisons the princess in it?" Dennis asked.

"Not the princess," said Aunt Molleen, trying to remember. She had reached the age at which old details reproach her from a great distance, known but unnamable. "Someone else is put in it. Your Uncle Flaherty might know."

"Does she ever get out?"

"A man is put in the tower. For nine days. But when he comes out, for all the rest of the world it is as if nine years have passed."

"Jeepers. All his people must be dead by then. Or moved away. Who would he be friends with?"

She shook her head. "I don't remember how it ends up."

"Well, I know how this mango ends up," said Dennis. "I'm going to eat it."

It is in the logic of things that Mike and Erica fall in love, though no one logical dares riddle it out. Love is magic. Oh yes, Erica is a held person and Mike a natural holder; and she knows that while

79

a man like this must stray from time to time he will adore her children without intermission as long as life lasts. He is a powerful man, dangerous to enemies but safe among his friends. She has known too many ineffectual men, this girl, not to prize a bold one. She saw him once, high up on the girders, late in the afternoon after the other unions had gone home, laying down decking with a few of his fellows and shouting in animal joy, shouting like a cowboy. And that moment will leave an impression, because it teaches Erica that while a grown female has to be a woman for the rest of her life, a grown male can act like a little boy at times yet seem perfectly in character. Yes, too, Erica has a sense of adventure. Marrying out of the family appeals to her as a way of challenging her mother's feat. So there are things to list in the wherefore of this romance, but only one cause: it's there.

So Mike did land Erica for dinner, and he got what he wanted, which was a really neat time. I like her, he would probably have told you, asked what he saw in her. She's good company. Mike believes in reasons for being attracted even less than I do. Attraction doesn't have reasons; attraction *is* the reason. They took a long walk in the park one Saturday, and the following Friday Mike took Erica to the theatre, at Dennis' suggestion. Little brother picked out the play: *Cabaret,* which he said was rather cultural, and certainly marvelous. Mike couldn't quite follow it, but Erica loved it; and they had reached the point of laughing at things that no one else thought were funny. Remarkably, Mike did not try to put the ace on Erica the first time he got inside her apartment, and never stopped dressing right and choosing his words for her, till he realized he was doing it spontaneously, out of respect, not out of necessity. And, while he is not the most perceptive lad alive, his instincts for drawing the broad view of things—for *comprehending,* let us say—are sound. So he knew he was making an effect. And he was smart enough to realize that themes of religion and culture are mere intrusions in the story of love, so he asked Aunt Molleen to stop nagging him about Jewish, enlisting Dennis' aid in an informal campaign to loosen the old lady up.

* * *

Sure, there speaks Mike, not I. Would I have given up our melodious old rhythms and quirky turns of tongue willingly? But a contemporary tale must bear contemporary sounds.

Mike knew that Erica's family would give her grief at the same time for the same reasons, came the day she at last told them about Mike, if she ever did, and perhaps she might not, for after all they were not necessarily . . . well. You know.

"Maybe they won't mind so much if they know I'm Irish," he joked, not joking. "I mean, Irish is the next best thing to Jewish, right?"

"Irish is the worst, actually," said Erica.

"What? Why?"

"Because the Irish are all drunken roughnecks who beat their children and abandon their wives. Hadn't you noticed that, you handsome boyeen, or whatever the term is?"

Mike said nothing.

"At least, if you were a WASP you'd have money. If you were Italian you wouldn't drink. If you were Russian you'd spoil your kids."

"I'm going to treat my kids right. I won't hurt them and I won't spoil them. I'll be the perfect father, because I'll teach them how to be good grown-ups."

She was thinking, You're the only man I've met about whom that is absolutely correct, and he saw her thinking it, and kissed her long and truly. That was the night they first made love, and I'm sorry to say that they presented a rather conventional twosome. After Dublin Johnny and his lessons in charm, and young Johnny and his professional lovemakers, and even Pete the Duke Reever and his arresting detours, we might find Mike and Erica almost boring, though they themselves were too intrigued with the prospect of getting to know each other to worry about the quality of their performance. People in love think they're terrific in bed.

And Erica noticed this: that while she had had crushes on various men, none of them had been as intently sexual as Mike.

81

The way he smiled at her when she opened her door, young as he was, was sheerly male—not intrusively seductive, not *playing* any part of romance or lust: just being it, all of it. Mike.

And Mike noticed this: that while sexually he had been, as 'tis said, around the block, he had never had a crush before, and thus the sense of poignant plundering he experienced in bed with Erica was disturbingly interesting.

And both of them realized, with a start, that they really must be in love, very deeply, very wonderfully, very pointedly, and they must now either agree to serve as the love of each other's life, or separate, and immediately. So, suddenly Mike was too Christian for Erica, a callow youth, a promising drunken roughneck; and Erica was too classy for Mike, snotty maybe, eventually, and always siding with her probably huge family that, come to think of it, Mike hadn't even met.

How could she bring an Irishman to meet her family, already carrying the shame—at times quite verbally—of her Christian mother, with her genes passing on who knew what sort of misbehavior and impiety? Not only an Irishman: a construction worker!

How could he so merrily take up with someone out of the neighborhood? Out of his kind?

They ran through these arguments daily, hourly, when they saw each other and when they didn't, when they were giggling, silly and touched, and when they felt the bite of possession so keenly they shocked themselves silent. Twenty times Erica had set out to meet Mike, swearing this was the last and knowing that it probably wouldn't be—next week, then: but next week they would be a week deeper in love and it would be yet harder to break apart.

Then this happened: Erica said they should try doing without each other for six weeks, and Mike said no.

"You can't say no," Erica told him.

"What do you mean do without each other? Why?"

"To see if we can."

"Why should we see if we can do a shitfool thing like that?"

The bad word told her he was mad. "Because if we can, we should."

Bewildered, but impressed by how quiet she was, he waited.

"Because," she continued, "sooner or later, we're going to have all sorts of trouble."

"No, we won't."

"We're like . . . like John of Arc and Willa the Conqueror."

"I don't know those guys."

"That's one of the troubles," she said dryly.

He sat next to her, to hold her, and she resisted, but he just wrapped her up and took her in, anyway. One of several advantages in being a man.

She cried, one of the disadvantages in being a woman.

"It's not good, Mike," she kept saying. "I know it isn't. I *know* it." Be true to your kind, we are taught, and we repeat it ourselves. Revere Tara, the House of Israel, fatherland. There is no world; there is only the neighborhood.

Such thoughts come handy when we fear to travel—but they are excuses, not credos. Mike believes this family argument to be silly, however much he has voiced it himself. But then his mother is dead, his father never seen, and his older brother not even mentioned. A man with only an aunt, an uncle, and a little brother can feel very cosmopolitan. If Mike were sophisticated as well, he would suspect that Erica has more on her mind than the tribulations of misalliance. She is not used to appetitive, swearing, jaunty men. She is not related to any, knew none in school, meets none in business. Yes, at first she was exhilarated. But there comes a moment when the wonderful package discloses, like a secret, the menace of an unfamiliar vitality.

He is a holding man, and she a held woman. For the moment, she can only let it be. But she has made up her mind. This night, they part. They must and will. This night.

"Are you going to stop crying?" says Mike.

"No."

Dennis was giving Mike trouble, too, staying out till all these late hours and talking like someone who just came back from a trip to the fairy kingdom or somewhere. Odd expressions came out of him, like blips of *Vogue*. And he had copped a gig to play piano at a party in Fire Island for an entire weekend. It seemed kind of fancy-dancy to Mike.

Even Aunt Molleen had her grouchy moments now. She was offended when Mike announced he was going to get a place of his own.

"I heard about them bachelor apartments!" she said. "You'll be taking the lovely foreign princess there!"

First she was going to cry, then suddenly got so gruff that Mike had to call Uncle Flaherty in to smooth everything down. But no sooner was Mike moved into his two tiny rooms over a Chinese take-out joint on East Seventy-third Street, than Erica set about vanishing from Mike's life. She refused to see him, and beseeched him not to call her anymore. If he did, she would hang up on him without a word. She *swore* she would; she *swore* it. Mike was pacing the place in fury when Dennis dropped in.

"What are you sore about?" said Dennis.

Mike told him.

And Dennis immediately had the solution: send her a letter so nice and wonderful that she'll have to change her mind. "Tell me about this romance," he urged, "and don't leave anything out. Then we'll see how to lure her out in the open."

"Do you have to put it like that?" said Mike—but he was already pouring out his tale: how they met, how they talked, how they first got to bed—and this last, when unexpurgated, is something brother tells only to brother.

"Pete Reever brought you together," Dennis noted. "Interesting."

"No, it isn't. He has nothing to do with it. Erica's in one world and Pete's in another."

"And which are you in?"

Mike looked at him. "Now what the hell is that supposed to mean? Because I can't help noticing that the one who's maybe trying to get from one place to another is you, do you know that?"

"Do you want help or do you want to yell at me?"

Mike grunted.

"Anyway. Now, what's the problem here? With Erica. What's the *base* we have to touch? You're certain she loves you, but she's backing out. That doesn't add up. Have you told me *everything?*"

"Yes!"

"There's a missing piece, then. Somewhere in this." Dennis was gazing pensively at Mike.

"What the fuck are you looking at?"

"You wouldn't happen to have paper and a pen, would you?"

Mike did.

"Graph paper and a mechanical pencil. I should have known."

"They work, don't they?"

Dennis started to write, in exactly the way Mike had seen him working out the lyrics to his songs at Aunt Molleen's: staring at the paper, at the walls, at Mike, unseeing, his finger pointing, teeth pushing on his lips, nodding when an idea seemed right, saying no out loud when he cancelled out words, making notes in the margins, rereading, rewriting, nodding again and smiling.

"Okay," said Dennis.

"Well?"

"Can you do three months without her?"

"Shit."

"Can you?"

"Why three months? Why not now?"

"Because I don't know the missing piece. If I did, I'd strike right there, and soothe that . . . that particular note. But I don't know it, right? I don't know it. So we have to play it more generally. Now, in love separations, the first six or seven weeks are the meanest. Utter doom. Then you start to wake up a little, joke around, date. You come out of it. Provided you don't see or hear from the other party, you'll recover in half a year or so. But. What if the other party is around somehow? Or, even worse, what if there's a hope of reconciliation? Then you can forget half a year, because you'll spend the whole time thinking of that other party, and getting back together, and you'll become miserable. Because then it's not what might have been, but what might yet be. Right?"

Mike stared at Dennis, trying to place somewhere in this seventeen-year-old the little boy who whistled codes with Mark Revien.

"How do you know so much about it?" said Mike.

"I'm a smart kid. Didn't you always know that?"

Mike nodded, put a hand on Dennis' shoulder. "So, in three months, what?"

"You're going to write her that you think parting is a big mistake, but you're going to accept her word for now. But you would like to see her one last time. She'll owe you that then."

"She owes me that now."

"Sure. But she may not give it to you now. Three months, Iron Mike. You meet her in the open, on the street, so she'll feel safe. Or so you'll say. Actually, what she'll feel like is gravy looking for roast beef."

Mike blushed.

"Because, look, if she really loves you, she is not going to find someone else in the next three months. Someone at all, maybe. But not someone better, or even as good. Three months from now she'll be out of her mind needing you. Maybe she'll tell herself she just wants to see you; sometimes they have to do that. She'll be lonely and vulnerable and you'll be calm and sweet and marvelous." He smiled. "Think you can manage that?"

"Is this going to work?"

"Now we have to pick a place of sentimental appeal. That'll really get her. And the date and time must be convenient."

Mike named the street where they first met. "Lunchtime."

"Let's do it on a Saturday. High noon, easy to remember. Make sure you're on time."

"Are you kidding? I'd better be. Erica is never late."

"Well, in this case, she'd wait for you, I somehow expect. And you can wear a suit."

"Huh?"

"We're going to buy you a new one. Something spiffy."

"Something *Vogue?*" said Mike.

Dennis blinked at him.

"Dumb joke," said Mike.

"Now you'll write this out, send it off, and get ready."

"What do I do for the next three months?"

"Do a lot of fucking."

They went out for pizza, and after a while Mike was almost ebullient.

Three months later, in a vested suit Dennis helped him pick out, Mike stood at the appointed corner ten minutes early feeling very much the nerdy dude; but women gave him the eye the way they never did when he was on the site. There's got to be something in this, he thought, fingering the vest buttons. The salesman kept unbuttoning the bottom one when Mike was trying it on and Mike kept buttoning it right up again. It was buttoned now. I'm probably not standing right or something, he guessed. They should give you suit lessons when you buy these things.

It was a rugged October day, sombre, clear, cold. Very New York weather, clever weather, fast-moving. Shoppers scuttled past Mike, some with what looked like a year's supply of something in huge illustrated bags, others bearing dainty Fifth Avenue paper pokes, as if they had bought a single cuff link or a jeweled tea bag.

11:56.

A baglady rushed Mike, screaming, "You stole my back issues of *Coronet*, you zombie!" but when he didn't budge she raced on, crying, "Zombies are coming! Hide your back issues! Evacuate the city! Zombies!"

Mike waited, trying to imagine what direction she'd be coming from. By cab, up Third Avenue. By subway, from Lexington and Fifty-first. Unless she had stayed over at her folks', which she sometimes did on Friday nights. Then she'd be coming down Park.

11:59.

He gazed westward, checking the collar of his coat to be sure it wasn't standing up. One minute more and we'll know. Erica is never late.

The Story of
LITTLE BROTHER

"Do you want to dance, little boy?" his mother would say, leaning on the Victrola, her finger smoothing out waves in time to the music, most often a waltz.

"Yes," he would answer, afraid she might suddenly snap back that he was too young, or too stupid, or just no. But sometimes she would turn to him and smile with great serious purpose, as if their dance would be a devotion of some kind, a penance. And she would hold out her hands to the child, and he would take them, and they would move through the parlor, his eyes fastened to hers. She would sing along.

> *One last waltz tonight,*
> *One to conclude the dance . . .*

She seemed, when they danced, to love him, him as he was. How she would smile! He felt sure of her, and would nod along, listening to the words as she uttered them, as if they were sharing sensible advice as they danced.

89

One last sweetheart's lie takes
One last hopeless chance . . .

No one else would dance with her, maybe, or no one else could.
She would not otherwise choose him, he knew. But she loved to
dance. After, when she turned the Victrola off, he would ask, "Do
you love me, ma?" And she would reply, "Love is the thing that
owns you, and you must never love, little boy."

"Don't you love my da?"

"Himself least of all, little boy."

"Do you love your own da?"

"I've none."

"Or anyone at all, then?"

She would say nothing to that. She'd look away, or shake her
head. But the little boy knew the answer. She loved one: his
brother Mike. She hid it as best she might, out of fear of the
father's jealousy. But a little brother, come last into it all, and
fresh, not being misled by old pacts made before the hearts
changed, would know. So the mother and son danced, knowing and
not saying, the hands touching, and the eyes. Her singing and him
nodding, in the front room, to the Victrola.

Sorry lovers swaying,
Sorry music, too . . .

That is Dennis Finn Keogh's oldest memory of his ma, or of
anything.

All his memories were of family, and of people who might easily
have been family: laughed, spoke, thought, celebrated, and sor-
rowed in the same patterns as Dennis' people. Time edged past him
not as history or experience or even as a succession of days and
nights, but as a choice of people to be with: his mother, dancing;
or his brother Mike, who let him hang around with the big kids;
or his sidekick, Mark Revien, a good pal for a tough neighborhood
because he was tall for his age and fought dirty. Dennis and Mark

would sit on Mark's stoop singing their own scabrous lyrics to popular songs, their voices growing loudest when girls of their class passed by.

One afternoon they put the word "fart" into every song, along with such attendant concepts as "smell" and "faint." They were giving an encore of a number from *My Fair Lady*, "Help Me Lay a Fart on Time," when Charlene Bono strode up to them, put her hands on her hips, and said. "From now on, you are the two most gross boys in the whole school!"

"What from now on?" asked Mark. "We always been!"

"I expect it of Mark, because he's a kike," Charlene went on. "But *you* ought to know better, Dennis Keogh!"

"Next we'll do that old favorite, 'You'll Never Fart Alone,' " said Dennis.

"Meanwhile, if I'm a kike," Mark observed, "you're a wop." Charlene took herself away with hauteur.

"I saw her finkie," Mark confided.

Dennis reckoned this must be some erotic bodily part, and said "Yeah," knowingly. He had already realized that one often gets along in the world by saying "Yeah" to things one does not understand. The members of one's family, for instance, must be tolerated though their actions are often incomprehensible. Dennis, too young for any Keogh to worry about what he tolerated or did not tolerate, would wait with Mark till Mike came by to pick him up. Without Mike, Dennis was afraid to be home.

Years later, people would ask him, "How did you get started in music?" and he would reply, "We had music in the house." The Victrola, the dancing. In fact, Dennis had to go in search of most of his music, hanging around record stores asking grown-ups to take him into listening booths to hear something until he was thrown out, sneaking into movie theatres through the exit doors to see musicals, even befriending kids whose parents had a television in hopes of lucking into a variety show. He most liked songs that told a story, or seemed a part of one; too many of his ma's records sang the same simple message over and over: love is sweet, love is sad, love is true. Dennis wanted to hear of other things.

He admired theatre music above all, for it was the richest sector in American songwriting. One Saturday afternoon Mike took him across town to the theatre district, so Dennis could see the places where his music was made. It was just before matinee time, and crowds of people scurried past them.

"This is definitely your better element of society," said Mike, unimpressed.

"How old do I have to be to see a show?" Dennis asked. "I'm almost ten already."

"You have to be rich, not old."

"Because I see some kids in this crowd."

"Rich kids."

They strolled through the thespian quarter, Dennis enthusing and Mike detached, grunting as Dennis read out the titles on the marquees and described the dramatic context of the photographs hung outside.

"How do you know about these shows since you never seen any?" Mike finally asked.

"I make it up."

Mike laughed.

"Iron Mike, will you take me to a show someday, when I'm a little older? I want to see some of these real fierce."

Mike beckoned him along with a tilt of his head.

"No, seriously, will you? Iron Mike?"

"Hey, pipe down with the Iron Mike stuff. That's only for the neighborhood."

"Will you take me to a show?"

"Yeah, well . . . someday." He shrugged. "It's not so great to go where rich people go, you know? It's not slick."

"I don't care about them."

"That's great, because they don't care about you. All they care about is using each other. Like a snake pit with a million snakes."

They crossed Fifth Avenue, Mike watching the world and Dennis thinking about it. This is why they got on so well: together they made one perfectly capable human being.

"Hey, you know what?" said Mike. "I'll ask Sneaky Pazillo about it. Your theatres and stuff. He's been in and out of every building in Manhattan. Got a piece of the Cloisters in his room."

"Say!"

"He's gotten into the U.N. so often he may have to become a country and join it, whattaya say?"

"Iron Mike!"

"Hey, did I tell you to lay off that? You want to say how you're glad someone did something for you, you look him in the eye and shake hands." Mike demonstrated, with the eye of a detective and the right hand of a cowboy. "See? You got to be slick to get respect. You can't go around goofing off, right? And it don't matter whether you're on Second Avenue or Broadway, either. You just move like everyone you like the most has their eye on you and is judging you by how you carry yourself. Got me?"

"Okay."

"That's how you'll get respect."

A pretty woman with a good ten years' seniority on Mike passed them, and Mike whistled so shrilly that she turned. Spotting them, she shook her head with irritation and walked on. Mike looked as if he had scored a bullseye of some kind.

"Iron Mike," Dennis whispered. "What did that lady think when she was looking at us?"

"She thought, There are two solid guys."

Mike strutted home, Dennis surmising that his brother was one part fool and nine parts hero.

Sneaky Pazillo came through very availably on the theatre trip. The game, he explained, was to mingle with the crowd outside at intermission and go back into the auditorium with them for the second act, calmly taking one of the empty seats at the back of the theatre. True, you'd miss the first act. "But who wants to spend the whole day in a theatre, anyway?" was Sneaky's answer to that. It also helped if you procured in advance a *Playbill* to carry for authenticity. It didn't matter which one, because you rolled it up with the front hidden; they all looked the same from the back.

"And you have to dress nice," Sneaky added. "All in all, gentlemen, it's a toot."

"You're a real jim dandy, Pazillo," said Mike.

"What if we get caught?" asked Dennis.

Sneaky shrugged. "They throw us out. What do they do, arrest us for trying to be cultured?"

They settled on *The Sound of Music*, at Sneaky's suggestion. "That's a good Catholic show, for the kid here. Lots of nuns, and then they climb every mountain at the end. I seen it three times already—back of the orchestra's always empty. Second-act that one and we won't have to go to Mass that week."

"We don't go anyway," said Dennis.

"Hey!" cautioned Mike. You're not supposed to talk about that, apparently. So Dennis said "Yeah," not understanding and not fighting.

The following Saturday, Mike and Dennis put on their church clothes as Nora played records in the front room.

"Iron Mike," Dennis asked, as his brother tied his tie for him, "what's a girl's finkie?"

"You be good or else."

"Look," said Johnny, coming into the bedroom holding a mouse by the tail. "Let's stick it somewhere for a surprise."

"Put it in the old man's cigar box," said Mike.

"He'd kill us," said Dennis.

"The hell with that. He's never home, anyway."

Johnny went into the other bedroom.

"Why can't I know what a finkie is?"

"I need help with this," said Johnny, coming back in with the cigar box. "Here." He gave Mike the mouse, which hung limply in the air. Once it squeaked. Johnny opened the cigar box and set it on the bed, holding the top of the box open. "Okay." Mike put the mouse among the cigars and Johnny snapped the top on. "How come you're dressed like that on Saturday? Somebody die?"

"Sneaky Pazillo and me are taking the kid to a show."

Nora had reached her favorite waltz, the dancing song, and smiled absently at her children as they crowded in to await Sneaky's tap on the buzzer.

One last waltz tonight,
One to conclude the dance . . .

Dennis danced with Nora, and she sang along and Mike watched them, solemnly, proudly. Johnny watched with an empty face.

"Tell me you forgive me, dear," Nora sang. Then she asked Dennis, "Do you want to dance, little boy?"

"I *am* dancing."

The record ended.

"You look so handsome, Parnell," Nora told Mike. "So grown up. Parnell Michael. She strokes his hair." And did so.

"We're going to the show, ma."

"You're taking the little boy?"

"I'm going to see—"

"That's good boys, and off with you, now." She looked at Johnny. "Not you, then?"

Johnny shook his head.

"Go, anyway. Find your father that you take after so fondly. Tell him I want to see him, perhaps some day before the Last Judgment, if he'd be so kind. And say to him that if he'd bring somewhat along for the household accounts, I'd not take it amiss."

Johnny stared at his mother, not moving.

Mike and Dennis left.

Sneaky had a *Playbill* for each of them to carry, and showed them how to mosey inside just behind the most prosperous-looking adults as if they were all together, and how to stand near likely looking seats till the lights were dying. Dennis was apprehensive about the ushers; he felt as if as if he were bearing a sign reading, We snuck in. But a smart little brother does what the big kids do; it's the fastest way to grow up. And the music began almost immediately, and the curtain shot up, and Dennis' senses of locale and season and self were sharpened and soothed at once. Following the story, studying the techniques of presentation, and simply enjoying the performances, he imagined he had come into a place in which everyone was a birthright native from the first moment. Dennis belonged here; there were not many places where he did.

95

And think: the city, the world, is full of theatres! You can come back forever.

"How did you get started in music?" they would say, interviewers, colleagues, strange people. Everyone wants to know where something begins, where a life was changed. But the more intent question is, How did you feel then? How Dennis felt was welcome. Whatever you may have done wrong in the past, and however others may have wronged you, and whatever you wanted and can never have, and what was taken from you irretrievably—all this, so elemental in the world outside, falls away in the eloquence and poignance and generosity of the theatre, in its ability to penetrate, to forgive. Some day, when Dennis is feeling impish, they'll ask, How did you get started in music? and he'll answer, "When Sneaky Pazillo and my brother Iron Mike smuggled me into the second act of *The Sound of Music.*"

"I don't want to leave," he said at the end, hunkered down into his seat, as the two older boys, on their feet and restless, beckoned to him.

"You got to leave," said Mike.

"I'm never going to leave."

Mike looked at Sneaky, who said, "Give him a noogie."

"What'd ma do," said Mike, "if I came home without you?"

"She'd say, 'Good, because I never liked him anyway.'"

"Come on, how is that to talk?"

It's true, Dennis thought.

"If you don't leave," ventured Sneaky, "the theatre guy'll come up and ask to see your ticket."

"All right," said Dennis, rising.

"That's the thanks I get," said Mike. "Hey, Pazillo, did you see the blonde with the big tits in front of us, on the aisle? When she left? She was rubbing them."

"She needs a friend to say hello to her and such," said Sneaky. "Some neat gentleman, I think."

"How'd you like to have balls big as those tits, huh?"

"Who says I don't?"

Outside, Dennis begged them to let him look at the pictures.

96

"Now you won't have to make it up about what they're for," said Mike, standing alongside him. "You won't need no one to take you around here anymore either, little brother. You're on your own."

"Here," said Sneaky, handing Dennis a *Sound of Music Playbill* he had picked up on their way out. "So you can come back all set up."

Dennis took it, looked Sneaky in the eye and held out his hand.

"You want a dime?"

"I want to thank you."

Sneaky shook Dennis' hand under the marquee of the Lunt-Fontanne Theatre.

"How's that, huh?" said Mike, clapping Dennis on the shoulder. "Did I raise him right?"

Dennis shook Mike's hand, too.

"He's a sport," said Sneaky, a connoisseur.

Dublin Johnny was in the front room when they got home, heavy and wet, sprawled on the couch as if he had been spinning around the room and then fell. The cigar box, open, was on the eating table. Nora and Johnny came in from the bedrooms when they heard the front door close.

"You," said Dublin Johnny to Mike.

"Go outside, Parnell," said Nora. "Aunt Molleen can give you supper."

"Go nowhere," said Dublin Johnny, struggling to his feet. "Aunt Molleen can wipe her hindparts with her supper."

Nora started forward, but Dublin Johnny pushed her back, commanding the room.

"I know you for a little blackguard and a weasel," he told Mike. "I know you for certain. Hear me, you turd?" Staggering, he grabbed the table; the cigars shuddered in the box. "You put a creature in my cigars," Dublin Johnny went on, incredulously. "I'll whip you for it, you bastard."

Mike shook his head slowly, impassively.

"You bastard," Dublin Johnny repeated.

"I did it," said Dennis.

97

"You're his little whore-follower," said Dublin Johnny, "so shut your mouth good and *shut* it and you just *shut it up!*"

"I put the creature—"

"No, he didn't," said Mike.

"You both did it, as you both do everything," said Dublin Johnny. "You stole life from me, from my loins, from my strength and love of the world. You'd have my flesh and vital organs and make a meal of me, the two of you." He pushed himself away from the table. "God will tell me what I did on this earth to deserve sons like you. When my time is called, and I go to settle the bill, He'll say, 'What have you done in your time, Dublin Johnny Keogh? What have you done for Tara?' And I'll say, 'Bejeezus, I must have done something deeply pernicious somewhere in it because otherwise *why did you give me those two bloody bastards for sons?*'" Whereupon he struck out and sent the cigar box flying across the room.

"I did it," said Dennis. "By accident."

Dublin Johnny came toward him. "Then I'll teach you how to be a finer man and avoid accidents, you fucking brat."

Mike pulled Dennis around to the far side of the table and held a chair up before his father. With a roar, Dublin Johnny went for him and they struggled as Nora shouted, "Stop them, Johnny! He'll murder someone, drunk as he is!"

"Stop them yourself, if you're so inclined," said Johnny, striding out of the apartment.

Drunk as he was, staggering and panting, Dublin Johnny easily overpowered Mike, and tossed the chair aside. Mike herded Dennis and Nora behind him toward his parents' bedroom, but Dublin Johnny caught up with him and they were grappling when Nora grabbed her husband by the head with her two hands and dragged him back, and screamed some wordless tattle and fell back, pulling him on top of her on the couch.

"Parnell!" she cried. "Go, now!"

Instead, Mike went to separate them, and Dublin Johnny heaved himself up with such force that he fell down again on the other side of the room. He lay on the floor, gasping, his body groaning. He was not yet fifty, but work and whiskey and the charming of a thousand women had aged him cruelly. He ran his hand over his face, licking his lips, and a ragged laugh came out of him. "Someone will pay for this, now," he said. "Maybe later, it's true, but someone will, and there's my oath on it."

"Little boy," said Nora. "Help your father up, now that the noise is done, thank heaven for something."

"He'll do no such," said Dublin Johnny. "No thankless brat'll raise up this lad." He struggled to his feet, and swayed, and looked like a cartoon whose caption was a curse.

"What have you to say at last?" said Nora. "You, not home these three weeks and now shaking the place down?"

"You sent the Johnny for me, did you not?"

"Not for this."

"Well." Dublin Johnny turned to Dennis, almost pleasantly. "What's cigars, anyway? A coffin in the nail of my dear old mother."

Dennis looked him in the eye and held out his hand.

"There's peace, then," said Nora, rubbing Mike's shoulders.

"Peace it is," said Dublin Johnny, taking Dennis' hand. "Peace," he said, grasping Dennis by the hair with his left hand. "I'll teach you what is peace," he said, smashing the boy across the face. Then he turned to Mike. "Now you."

"What's this again?" said Nora, spitting in fury, barring Mike's way. "Oh, what's this for us, now?"

Dublin Johnny smiled. "I'll have satisfaction of the two brats for what they did."

"Not this one," said Nora.

Dennis was staring at Mike.

"The both," Dublin Johnny said. "For they are a pair of traitors to the name of Keogh."

And Nora, shielding Mike with her body and keeping him safe with her spread arms, seemed just then about to say a thing in reply, something relative to the notion of the name of Keogh. At length she said nothing—but a secret flickered in her eyes, and Dublin Johnny and Dennis both saw it. Mike, behind her, did not.

99

Dublin Johnny seemed to go slack for a moment, and once again the fight appeared over. Then he took hold of Dennis by the neck, pensively, perhaps experimentally. "Hand that one beyond," he told Nora, "or I give this one the beating of his days."

Now, without a word, Nora takes hold of Mike in ferocious embrace, and he cannot cut free. Dublin Johnny is still, watching them, and he laughs. He does not seem drunk anymore. "You see how it is," he says to Dennis. "You see them together. She loved me like that once."

And he pushes Dennis into the bedroom, locks the door behind him, and beats the boy savagely.

Surely it was not long before Mike fought Nora off and broke into the room. But, even that soon, it was over: Dublin Johnny was sitting on the bed, a fat and scroungy old loser; and the window was open, and Dennis was gone.

Mike turned the neighborhood inside out till he remembered the hunter's secret of thinking like the quarry, and hied himself to the Lunt-Fontanne Theatre to wait for *The Sound of Music* to finish its evening performance. First out were the smart suburban jokers, racing to the garages, then some chic uptown aisle-sitters, then the ponderous mob who reach a hit show in its shabby last months and sit before it in the opaque joy of the cultural zombie. Then came the dizzy idlers, wandering off to some bistro, then the stragglers who had dropped a glove or met a friend. Last came Dennis, his face bruised but his eyes shining. He spotted Mike and stopped a few feet away.

"I didn't cry," said Dennis.

Mike came up to him. "I'm sorry, little brother. I tried to be there."

"I know."

"And, look, you don't have to stand up for me. I can take care of the old man. That was really dumb."

Dennis nodded.

"It was a true thing, though. To do it. No kidding, Dennis, you're a man now. You really . . ."

"Is he still there?"

"Who the fuck knows? We're going to stay with Aunt Molleen."

"Did you see how I got out the fire escape?"

"Yeah, that was neat."

"You—"

"Listen—"

"—knew I was here."

"You aren't sore at me are you?"

Dennis shook his head.

"I won't let him catch you again, little brother. I promise."

"Sure."

"He doesn't come around much anymore, anyway."

"Sure."

"No, listen, I promise. Okay?"

"Sure."

"That fucking Johnny set us up."

"Iron Mike."

They were holding each other and crying.

There is trouble in a family when a secret is exposed. Even if it be a secret pro forma, a thing known but never mentioned, it may be ignored, forced out of thought, very nearly *un*known. But to utter the dread feelings, or to reveal them through some impulsive act, will make necessary certain renegotiations in the family contract.

Thus it was that Dennis came to live with his Aunt Molleen. There was no overt announcement, no decision apparently made. "Perhaps it's best," said Nora, when Mike came back to his mother's house leaving Dennis behind.

Dennis thought it best, partly because Aunt Molleen had a piano. She played a quite decent Irish Parlor Keyboard, and took the time to help Dennis pick out songs he liked with a rudimentary chording. One day he figured his way through "Moon River" by himself, and practiced it, and played it for Mike, and shook his hand. At last, Dennis thought, I really am growing up.

How else can you be sure, unless you change your habits? You can't change your family, even if you emphasize an aunt; and such other factors as region and language are immutable, at least in the lives of the Keoghs. You can change your friends, true: but Dennis hadn't had the chance yet. Mark Revien and he still palled around on the local stoops, Charlene Bono continued to chide Dennis' betrayals of tone in the neighborhood's Irish-Italian Catholic alliance, and half the kids with him in seventh grade had been there when he had begun first grade in another building a few blocks away. He went to the theatre often, on the Pazillo plan. In all, he was just getting older, not growing up.

So it was the piano that aged him, as the only thing that was entirely his own. Aunt Molleen promised to leave it to him in her will.

Sometimes Mike would come to take him home for a visit.

"Why do I have to go?"

"It's your family, little brother. You don't have any choice."

"Oh yes, I do!"

"You be good or else. Once you have a family, they own you for life whether you like it or not."

Nora would have the Victrola going when they came by. Dublin Johnny and Johnny were never around.

"Some family," said Dennis.

"Do you want to dance, little boy?" asked Nora.

"No."

"Come on, my Johnny." She held his chin delicately. "The lad is shy, to make his charm the grander."

Mike had said she was acting funny.

"Aunt Molleen," Dennis said later, "can I ask you something?"

She nodded. "It'll be about your ma, surely."

"Yes."

"No. Then no. Don't ask me nothing. Play some more of that piano for me while I take my tea. Just play music, my boy. Esh, a woman loves a man who plays the music. You'll see soon enough."

Dennis began "One Last Waltz."

"Isn't that from your ma's record?"

Dennis broke off and asked, "Why does a woman love a man who plays music?"

"Faith, has the boy heard different?"

"You know what I heard?" Dennis whipped around on the stool. "I heard a woman loves a tough man, Aunt Molleen. Like my da."

"Terrible news." Sipping her tea: ironic? bored?

"Is it true?"

Mike came in.

"Play us a tune, sport," he said, his hand on Dennis' shoulder, watching the keys. "Make that ivory dance."

It was another going-to-ma night. Dennis played "Blue Tango" and "How Can Love Survive" and "Knowing When to Leave" and everything else he could think of, until he ran out of numbers and Mike took him home.

"Dance with me."

"No."

She put the record on.

"Dance, little boy."

"See?" Dennis told Mike. Then, to Nora: "I'm not little anymore."

Sorry lovers swaying . . .

"No."

Tell me you forgive me, dear . . .

Johnny came out of the bedroom, rumpled from a nap.

"It's himself," Nora said. She chuckled.

"No, ma. Da is himself."

"My boys come to love me. My sons, all at once."

Johnny shook his head slowly as Mike got Nora to sit.

"Will he be coming?" she asked. "I've been waiting."

The record needle brushed against the back grooves with a rhythmic, repetitive *grssh*. Mike took the record off.

"If he comes," she said. "If he comes." She chuckled again.

"Go out, you both," said Johnny. "I can take care of her. You don't know about it."

"Tell us, then," said Mike, "and we'll know."

"Will he be coming?" Nora asked Johnny. "I fixed his coat for him."

"I'll get you a cup of tea, ma," said Johnny.

"I've had my tea."

"Why don't you go?" Johnny insisted.

"Why don't you like us?" said Dennis.

"My boys around me. Tea. His coat."

"I'll put your record on again, ma," said Johnny.

"We've as much right here as you," said Mike. "We live here."

"*He* doesn't."

"I used to," said Dennis.

"Sometimes she gets like this."

The music. They listened in silence, except Nora, who sang.

At the end of it, Dennis said, "I'm going to write music now myself."

"Write us a lovely waltz," said Nora, brightly. "That's what folks need, is a sweet tune to cheer them sadly. To remind them of love and soothe them." She thought. "Something quite sensitive. Will you?"

Everyone looked at Dennis, and he thought of Maire Dreeley's little boy, just able to walk, and how she was out walking him and when they passed Dennis and Mark Revien, sitting and singing, and Mark asked the child, "What's your name, little baby?", the boy turned and wobbled into his ma's arms and pressed against her so no one might find him.

"I will write 'A Waltz for My Mother,'" said Dennis at last.

"That's a fine boy, then," said Nora, gazing fondly about her and meeting no one's eyes. "All of you growing up so handsome, the girls'll be making the magic to fetch you." Her eyes rested on Mike, and his met them. "Your dark hair . . ."

* * *

"When she was a babe, she was troublesome," said Aunt Molleen of Nora. "Then she was a wild girl, then your da's wife and
your ma. And now she's wild again. It's the girl's frenzy in her
coming out whether we like it or no. Now, what are you playing?"

"A new song," said Dennis.

He would cross the street to avoid Johnny, but Johnny would catch
him to talk, if only for a moment. Sometimes Johnny was like their
father, impatient and disappointed; and sometimes like Nora, ne-
glectful and repentent.

"Don't say I don't like you anymore," Johnny told Dennis. "I
like you as much as Parnell does."

Dennis thought of the mouse in the cigars and how Johnny
tricked them, and Johnny read him, because your family knows
everything about you. Johnny grabbed Dennis by the collar and
said, with his eyes, That was for Parnell, not you. With his mouth
he said, "Don't you take off on me!"

Dennis made a leap, but Johnny whirled him around and bent
his arms behind his back. Dennis yelped in pain.

"Shut up," Johnny whispered, "or I'll bust it off you, I swear."

"Oh look, it's the roughnecks again, who make everyone think
this is a bad neighborhood." This from Gilda Bono, Charlene's
older sister, who had a sort of crush on Johnny.

"We're brothers playing," said Johnny, putting his free hand on
top of Dennis' head.

"Play in the parks, not in the streets," Gilda advised them. "As
Father Doyle says."

"Brothers play everywhere they go," Johnny replied.

"Dennis is crying," said Gilda. "Why is Dennis crying, if you're
playing?"

"It's part of the game," Johnny told her.

Gilda looked at Dennis. "It is?"

"Sure. Whattaya think?"

"I think you're hurting Dennis. Dennis, are you all right?"

105

Dennis nodded.

"Is it a game?"

Dennis nodded again.

She backed away a step and regarded them. "Your family is the talk of the town. And what are you doing now, I wonder, please?"

Johnny loosened his grip on Dennis and patted his head again. "See?" he said. "It's one of our jokes."

"I'd better go," said Gilda, staying put.

After a moment, Johnny said, "I have to talk to him," and Gilda went away.

"You listen to me, Dennis," he began. "We're the two brothers. You and me. Parnell is someone else. You know what I mean." He turned Dennis around to face him. "From another family. Another *father*. You know what they call children like that? He doesn't even look like us. Da doesn't know. Do you want me to tell him?"

"*No!*"

"Then listen!"

"Don't tell him! *Ever!* You'll just make more problems."

"Why don't you ever call me my name?"

Dennis looked at him.

"You call Parnell by that jerk nickname and you—"

"All right! Just don't—"

"What is it?"

"Dublin John Keogh, Jr."

"Say it like you were talking to me. *Johnny.* Say that."

Dennis looked up at his brother, tall and broad like their father, and from another world. No, the same world: Dennis was the alien. "You say you'll break my arm and then you—"

"I didn't mean it."

"You can't—"

"Listen—"

"You *can't.*"

Gilda Bono saw Dennis cry, and now everyone in the neighborhood will know. When you come home, you tell what you saw in the street.

"I'm sorry." Johnny rubbed Dennis' arm. "You made me sore. Why did you cross the street when you saw me?"

"What's wrong with Nora? Why is she like that?"

Johnny looked away. "I don't know, Dennis."

Dennis looked away, too, but he felt Johnny's eyes burning into him, so he turned back and said, "Well, don't talk about Mike anymore. It's the way it is. It's the family, now. If you make trouble, everyone will hate you."

Johnny smiled. "Not da, Dennis. Not da." He started for him, but Dennis raced away. "Listen to me! I'm sorry I hurt you! Dennis! Come back! I like you as much as he does! *Dennis!*"

Dennis kept running.

"Look at how tall you are, now," said Aunt Molleen. "And eating my table out of the house itself. Come play that new song for me again. I like to hear you sing it."

"I don't sing very well."

"But you have the spirit in you. You say the words as if they was pictures, and that's all enough. Come, now. Give it here again."

"This is called, 'Now I'm Running.' "

"Running, is it?"

Mike sometimes stayed over at Aunt Molleen's, saying only that "She wasn't herself today" or so. Dennis and Mike would lie together and talk themselves to sleep. Like journalists, they never ran out of conversation.

"What do you hear of da?"

"You ought to go running to your ma, maybe," says Aunt Molleen. "If now you're running."

"It's always trouble with her now."

"Trouble? You say this, Dennis Keogh? Mary and Joseph, to her sister in blood?"

"There's always a scuffle at hers."

"You'll not turn from son to nephew in this bailiwick, my fine man! You'll have enough to repent of one day without laying desertion of your ma to the account as well!"

Yet Dennis, that boiling summer afternoon, stood before his mother's door unable to enter. The building was strangely still, vacant and sullen, waiting for better times and the money and the new people to smash and rebuild and take over the neighborhood. At the top floor, Dennis looked down the stairwell. No one. But he heard noises in his mother's apartment, odd scratching sounds and confrontational murmurs . . . or, no, a light pounding and a fast, shouted question. Then the heavy pounding of something light, weak, unresisting. Da's voice, perhaps, somewhere in it.

Dennis approached and put his head to the door.

In the silence, Dennis heard a clatter of things and a cry of "Parnell!" as from a banshee disrupting a chess game.

Dennis slipped back down the stairs. He didn't like a scuffle; some men do. He thought he'd come back later.

Later she was gone. She was dead. She had been killed.

The collapse of a family seems most final when death is most unexpected—for there is no time to prepare to recover, to calculate how best to forgive one's relations for surviving. We blame ourselves somewhat, everybody else more enthusiastically. And Nora had been the very center of the Keoghs, distractedly and painfully but also absolutely, because she was the only one that the other four all loved. She herself was the kind who love one thing at a time, and so she had loved Dublin Johnny, and then she had loved Mike, and then she was dead at the bottom of the stairs, and that was her life. She did nothing else by choice, or well. She had not even the Church, not God, not a willing place in the Holy City. Nor was she avenged, for the police at length took her murder for accidental death by falling.

"She was redeemed by her children," said Aunt Molleen at the wake; one of those things you say to feel less final about a tragic case: He left something behind, or She planted a seed, or They made miracles possible. One says these things in the hope that your survivors will say them when your time comes, or that they will be true.

After the wake Dublin Johnny went off to wherever it was he was living now, and Johnny, with scarcely a look about him, went too. Mike moved in with Dennis at Aunt Molleen's, but he was seldom around there till bedtime, for his high school years were upon him, and there was always something for him to do with a crowd of people.

Suddenly alone, then, Dennis concentrated on writing songs. As Aunt Molleen took her tea, Dennis scratched out lyrics on yellow pads and fingered tunes for them, and she would say, "That's a sweet one," when she enjoyed it and "It sounds opera to me" when she didn't. How easy she was to like, and how easily she liked back. Dennis was lonelier than a boy his age should be, but writing made him feel powerful, because you could turn your rough feelings into sweet ones in a song. You might even keep them rough, for they didn't hurt as much when you sang about them.

Now, here is a thing: when he had forty songs, Dennis went through them and took out the lame and empty ones. Twenty-four were left, which is the number of fairy hounds that looked on unobserved when the King of Tara played chess with the Scornful Witch of Fooley. And that twenty-four, Dennis noted, were all concerned with the danger in the passion of families. An accident; still. Dennis resolved to write no more on such matters.

He launched a cycle to be called "Songs of Independence." It was the end of the 1960s, and the sound of Dennis was quite modern, a soft-rock cabaret, though he would often infuse the accompaniments with the effects of the old days, of the Peabody and the Black Bottom and barrelhouse swing and the Cannonball. Never a waltz.

"I'm going to be a songwriter, Aunt Molleen," he said one night at the piano, with his pencils and pads.

"Faith, you are one. What you're going to be is paid for it."

"That I am," he replied, in Irish for once.

Songs of Independence. For he had decided not to be forgiven, after all. Not to want to be, really. And that is the true power, the growing up: not to need anyone's certification.

"Iron Mike, listen," he would say, and sing one of his new songs.

"It's great, sport," said Mike, not getting it. "Are you going to sing them yourself?"

Dennis laughed. "I'll write them. *They'll* sing them."

Mike nodded. "Yeah, but who?"

"Everyone."

Yeah, but how? How to connect with that world? They make it difficult, Dennis reasoned, to discourage the cranks. Once they see that a fellow is of the true, they let him in. On his way home from the theatres he would pass the places where the great and near-great made party, and saw the clothes and entourages and lists on clipboards and lines of the neglected strung out against the walls. He would pass homeless crazies shopping in trash baskets or giving lectures in the plazas of the office towers on Sixth Avenue. He passed the black prostitutes on Lexington Avenue, rushing off whooping with laughter as a squad car screeched up. On Third Avenue, old bums shuffled out of the pubs muttering fey curiosa, and at last Dennis was home, Aunt Molleen asleep and Mike, in his pants, studying blueprints. "Don't I get a smile?" he asked, looking up.

"Iron Mike, how do I sell my songs?"

Mike thought. "Send them to the singers you like and expect a miracle."

"How do you send something to a singer? They must get tons of mail they never see."

"Don't they have a foreman or a manager? Something?"

"A producer."

"Yeah, okay. Send your songs to producers."

Dennis considered this.

"Send your songs to producers in care of the record companies," Mike went on. "Make it look real slick. Professional. You know what snobs those people are. And you should copyright them to protect yourself."

"How?"

"You write 'copyright' and your name on the bottom of every page. So what do they know, right? Maybe you really did register them with the feds and maybe you didn't. But if you did, and they steal your songs, you sue them, see?"

" . . . yes."

"It took you all that time to give me a smile? What am I, a goon?"

I know who your father is, Dennis thought, fighting the memory down.

He followed Mike's advice, and sent lead charts, lyric sheets, and cassettes. Nobody reads out there; everything is tape. Gilda Bono's husband, who worked in a recording studio, made the tapes at Aunt Molleen's, walking around like a Martian with a walkie-talkie something on his head and hanging wires over Dennis' shoulders. "Piano's out of tune" was all he said the whole time. Then Mike brought over a girl he had known in high school, because she could write the labels in semi-Gothic script in India ink, "to make them notice you," Mike said.

"Your brother has the fashion," Aunt Molleen commented after Mike and the girl had left to go dancing. "He'll never be lonely, that's certain." She insisted on paying the postage to California, and waited more avidly than anyone.

Some of Dennis' packages vanished like pennies in a well. Some came back, blank as taken pawns. A few, after quite some while, were returned in letters that asked, What else can you do?

What do you want?, Dennis thought. That's what I'll do. Except waltzes.

Grim Johnny Keogh rose when Dennis came in, on the last day of the school year. Aunt Molleen and her tea. Johnny in a beard.

"I want to talk to you," said Johnny.

"No."

"Now, is that any way?" asked Aunt Molleen.

"Leave us be," said Johnny.

"Well, I've had my cup, so I'll do the market."

"No," said Dennis, going to the door.

Johnny went for him and flattened him against the wall. "You'll hear me or I'll take it out on that other one." He sounded tired.

"He'd tear you apart!"

"I'd like to—"

"Take your hands off that boy," Aunt Molleen told Johnny. "You'll be calm in here, or on the street in an instant. Esh, the brothers! 'That other one,' is it?"

Johnny still held Dennis.

"And alike as two checkers," said Aunt Molleen, fretting, digging in her bag. "I've lost my lace, now. Here." She blew her nose. Johnny backed away and she looked at Dennis. He nodded and she left.

"Are we brothers," said Johnny, breaking the silence, "or not?"

"Maybe you are. I'm out of it."

"You're not out of it till you're dead." Family rules. "Now, come with me. To see da."

"No."

Johnny loomed over him. "You have to."

"Or what?"

After a moment, Johnny put his hand on Dennis' neck. "Come because I ask you. I'll never ask you for anything again. What a cheap bargain, Dennis."

"Where is he?"

"I have a car."

"No, *where?*"

"Are you coming quietly or not?" Grabbing hold of him again, the ruffian. "Nothing's going to happen to you."

"Everytime I do something in this family something happens to me," said Dennis, starting to gulp. "Why are you so hard? Why do you always make me cry?"

Johnny took his arm and led him to the street. "You're the hard one," he said, in the car.

Dublin Johnny was lying in bed in a rat hole in deepest Brooklyn. His right shoulder was bandaged and a near-empty bottle of whiskey perched on a blanket between his legs.

"Here's a surprise," said Dublin Johnny. "He came. Give us a hand and think kindly on your people. I'm not ready for the Father yet, but the feeling came upon me to give you my blessing now, and you know I like to do a thing when I think of it. Give us your hand, I say."

Dennis shook his father's hand.

"You failed me, boy. I'm not one for kind words even to his son. The truth is better. You failed me. You're my flesh and blood and I tried to love you, but you're all wrong, some way. She was strange to me at the end . . ."

He was rambling drunk, stabbing out ideas with authority but hesitant between the sentences.

"I think of her still, as she was. You aren't living in the streets, are you, like an orphan, or in some bastard priestly orphanage? . . . as she was, dancing."

The music, see?

"She was a girl fit for courting. You had to court her, your ma."

Dennis felt Johnny moving up to stand next to him. Two sons at the bedside.

Johnny put his hand on Dennis' shoulder. Dublin Johnny took a long drink and a long look, the empty bottle dropping to the floor and his head up slow to contemplate the two young men.

"You failed me, Dennis. That's of no account, now. I'm seeing you, as I wished to, and I say this: if you need help of any kind . . . there's certain things only your family can do for you. After I'm gone, if so it be, it's Johnny you're to look to. He's head of the Keoghs now, or will be. You see that, Dennis. After all this scuffling, you see it at last. Do you see it, Dennis?"

Dennis looked at Johnny, who almost smiled at him. How far back can you remember? Do you recall his lullabies? And the army of mice?

"We're falling away. It's the age, I know it. The family's not what it was. Not a pure thing, now. I want to see that you consent, Dennis." The slurring and rasping had grown gentle, rhythmic, soothing. "Consent and admit, Dennis. I want to see that you are for us. That you won't fail us anymore."

Now, with one thing and another, Dennis knew that he did not like these two men. That was his choice. But yes, as it is said, one is in for life. We can bear a grudge against a lover, a friend, the brutish grocery clerk or impenetrable super or even a stranger, and it can ripen into a fond hatred with time, like a fig, sweetening as it rots. But family grudges are a snare growing tighter by the hour, and which of us, offered the chance to pacify one in an act of self-redemption, will thrust it aside? Dennis looked Johnny in the eyes, and they were burning: so that when Dennis held out his hand to his brother, and his brother took it to pull him close and hold him, Dennis felt he had been drawn into a fire, and held his brother tightly, wishing that the heat would cool, and hating him, and needing this.

Not till Johnny drove him home did Dennis speak: "Is he dying?"

"He's bad off in other ways. The wound'll heal."

"How'd he get it?"

"Don't think about it and don't talk about it. To *nobody.*"

"I'm better off not knowing."

"That's for sure," said Johnny. "Just keep your mouth shut. You don't know nothing."

They rode in silence.

"Have you got a girl?" Johnny finally said.

"No."

"Why not? At your age."

"Because I'm going to screw men."

"That's a crummy joke at a time like this." Johnny stopped at Aunt Molleen's corner. "You're the hard one," he said, as Dennis got out.

Writing music was like going to the theatre, a form of consolation and enlightenment. Songs of liberation. And to pursue success might take one into the higher liberation of show-biz bohemia.

Also, it was easier than working. Dennis wrote a song called "Easy to Do."

Also, it was a way of leaving this and any other neighborhood of rivalry and resentment and death. Dennis wrote a song called "Dating Myself."

Also, it was something wonderful to think about, prospects, and Dennis wrote "Living in the Future."

Then he thought it was absurd to write so many driving, nervously intrepid songs in the first person, as these all were, when everything in the world inspired in him such mixed feelings. There were regrets in the most insistent fascinations, resentments toward the people one never tired of being around, needs as well as terrors of need, both at once. Dennis wondered if he ought to write at least one utterly defeated song, and thought of the title he had promised Nora, "A Waltz for My Mother."

No, let's not get personal. Let's imagine. Dennis saw himself as the playfully disgruntled pianist-singer in some midwestern dive. "The Maestro," he pencilled in, "of a Mellow Cabaret." Underlined it. Thought of a lazy blue vamp, plenty of black notes, come open up the keys. Played it. And wrote:

> *The lighting's on the dim side.*
> *The alcohol's a joke.*
> *The faces press around me,*
> *The whispers and the smoke.*
> *And I'm just what I seem, girls:*
> *A dreamer for you dream girls,*
> *The maestro of a mellow cabaret.*

First A. Not enough love. Everything is about love. And put some downtown in it.

> *My ballad makes them tender.*
> *My torchy number heats*
> *The passion of this fan club*

115

> *Of divorcees and cheats.*
> *No, they don't bring their dates here.*
> *Because their fate awaits here*
> *With the maestro of a mellow cabaret.*

Second A, Dennis testing the scan at the piano. The rhymes are too tricky but the tune will carry it. He'll go up on *fate*, high note for the singer, whoever. Dennis as a singer and girls' heart-throb: a neat joke, neat art, neat fascination without regret. The release:

> *The ladies seem to dig my performance*
> *As they cluster around the grand.*

Dig. Dated. But real downtown. Downtown's everything that got left behind when everything new sprang up. Downtown's what a million snakes can see from their balconies.

> *They'll ask for a scotch,*
> *A favorite tune,*
> *And an order of one-night stand.*

Last A now, a taste of the upbeat, with regret merely brushing in:

> *I'm here to soothe your spirits,*
> *To stroke your keening heart*
> *With promises and romance*
> *And sentimental art.*
> *It hurts to be so giving—*
> *But, hell, I make my living*
> *As the maestro of a mellow cabaret.*

Well, I don't know, who said you were supposed to write true to life?

And Dennis packed his new songs off to the record producers who had responded to his earlier songs. Aunt Molleen launched some very serious prayer on his behalf, and Mike took to saying, "Well?" about the mail.

Dennis did not mention his meeting with their father in Brooklyn, and certainly never considered setting it to music.

The mail, when it came, was bewildering. Contracts, options, something something offered as of something whatsoever, title fee (see rider attached) if not cancelled by act of God or Clive Davis, something not negotiable if something, attendance required at sessions if desirable, all this on papers of various sizes and colors in duples and triples. A thin envelope inside the other envelopes contained three checks written against staggered dates.

"Who said there's nothing in praying?" Aunt Molleen exulted. "Mary and Joseph!"

Dennis was not dazed; he felt frisky. "Okay," he said, "everybody gets a present. What'll it be?"

"You're a fine boy, Dennis. You'll make some true luck for us all at last, I'm certain. I'd like to see some Keoghs living for life instead of suffering." She was examining the checks. "These fine bits of paper pertain to banks in California, so I think I've the time to indulge in some old-fashioned Sligo gloating before I choose my present."

"I'm going to find Iron Mike."

"That's right. Good news stings till you share it with your friends. You'll be remembering how it felt now, so when they ask you, years from this, you can tell them. And your brother'll be bragging to his gang, I expect, won't he? It's like having babies!"

It was always "your brother" now, just the one. Johnny had dropped from sight. Person by person, the family was losing its history.

Mike's crew had left the site by the time Dennis got there, so he made a fast tour of the local pubs to find him. As he walked into Carney's, someone grabbed his face by the hand, none too gently: Mike's sometime buddy Pete Reever.

"Well, look at little brother."

Dennis had to pull on Pete's arm to free himself. Pete smelled of beer; but so did the neighborhood, generally.

"Hey, Pete. I'm looking for Iron Mike."

"He's a good man. Your brother is a fucking good man."

Shoot, he's blasted. They should raise the drinking age for ironworkers to sixty.

"C'mere," said Pete, pulling Dennis deeper into the bar. "Want you to meet some—"

"Pete, I've got to find Iron Mike. It's major."

"Well, I'll help you, man. Don't get your donkey wrecked. You'll live longer." He pulled Dennis' arms out of the bar and the rest of Dennis followed. "You tried Clancy's? Parnell's?"

"Don't you ever wear a shirt?"

"In this hot?" Pete tickled Dennis' neck just where the hair ended. "Hey, little brother."

Dennis looked at him, the smiling man, the setter. Growing up the last of three, Dennis had reckoned how to get along with men larger than himself, including the outraged and the desperate and the implacable: be neither arrogant nor humble. Be like the New Yorkers with briefcases, late for an appointment with the rest of your life. Look sturdy, move quick.

"Come on," said Pete. "We'll hit every gin mill in the place!"

And have a beer in every one, Dennis thought, just now feeling the kick of what had happened to him. Contracts and money and entree! No doubt he would have to sign over royalties to some crook, but it was worth anything to get in. He could always write more songs.

"The hell with it," said Pete, stopping at the most debased brownstone on Fifty-first Street. "Come upstairs. I want to show you something."

An odd thought struck Dennis; Pete touched his neck again. "Come on," he urged. "This is a good time."

Realizing that this was true, that one must break in somewhere, the way you study blueprints or send your songs to producers or walk into Dublin and ask, Dennis followed Pete upstairs. At the door, Pete flashed a grin at Dennis and said, "Here you go" as he pulled open the door, and I feel these are very knowing words, for through that door Dennis passed into his fate. Like, I am sure, my readers, I wish he strode more ambitiously toward his goals; he seems at times to be letting prevailing winds blow him whither he goes. Perhaps, after passing so much energy to Johnny and Mike, the combined afflatus of Keogh and of Flaherty gave out before Dennis came along. Tara suffers from—among other afflictions—a disorderly gene pool. But we've no shortage of poets, though their quality greatly varies.

"I could never show these to your brother," said Pete, picking up a stack of something. "He's all tightened about delicacies. They're supposed to be his saintly mother or something."

Pete showed Dennis photographs of himself and a woman.

"Christ, it's hot," said Pete, pulling off his pants. "Make yourself comfortable and you'll get used to it."

"Who took these?" asked Dennis.

There were several shots in which the woman, in a maid's cap and bearing a rolling pin, held an accusing finger at Pete, who stood covering his genitals with his right hand and, head down, tried to look penitent. Another series offered Pete perched more or less on the woman's knee, his cock fiercely erect as she, in glasses, read from *The Little Engine That Could.*

"Art studies," said Pete, lighting up a joint.

Dennis wandered over to Pete's window and looked down a small airshaft. Outside it was still sunny, but no light flew into Pete's room. "Nice view," said Dennis.

Pete handed Dennis the joint. "Sometimes I throw stuff down there."

"Good place to dump your secrets."

"You aren't doing it right. Got to inhale it in real deep. Right down to your cock." Pete put his arm around Dennis' waist. "Didn't your brother teach you to smoke right? Uncle Pete'll show you. A toke should make you tingle, don't you know that? Watch me." He drew on the joint, a finger outlining the smoke's trip into his system down the center of his torso. "All the way down. See? Try again, now." Dennis inhaled too much of the stuff and

119

coughed. Pete shook his head. "Wasting good toke. "I'll show you." He slipped Dennis' T-shirt off and opened his pants like a pickpocket. "Yeah." As he pulled down Dennis' shorts, Dennis wondered if every first time is a seduction by your big brother's big buddy. "Try it again, nice and easy. Take it in . . . relax . . . be content. I'm going to show you a real nice game." Pete's finger followed the smoke down Dennis' chest and traced a pause at the rim of his pubic hair. "Feel it tingle now, little brother? You're learning fast." He rubbed Dennis' neck again. "Your brother should be teaching you these things, so you don't make a fool of yourself with the ladies. He ever show you how to make a lady? I bet he didn't. Old Mike doesn't like playing the hotshot, does he? Now, the best way is to honeybunch 'em. Sweet talk. Because what a lady's afraid of, is you'll be rough. So you got to touch 'em real nice, like this, and whisper in their ear." Pete whispered, "I really want you to trust me. Will you trust me and let me make you content?"

He gazed at Dennis, waiting for him to answer.

"Who am I in this?" asked Dennis.

"You're Mike Keogh's little brother, learning how to taste ladies. How to talk to them and get them down. Right?"

Dennis reached up and grasped Pete's shoulders and spoke his name.

"That's nice," said Pete. "I'm just trying to show you how to do it, because you can't use tough words. You got to frame your code, like . . . 'I sure would like to lay you, honeybunch.' Or 'I bet you would look pretty lying back on this bed here. Will you let me see that?' " Pete drew Dennis to the mattress. "I want to show you the new position that all the ladies love, real delicacy." Pete stretched him out on his back. "They're real content to be put in this position, because it's real sincere. That's the ticket with the ladies, being sincere." Pete stroked Dennis, held his eyes with his own, smiled and nodded. "Saw this in an after-hours place once. A sex club, you know? Guy with this big monster donkey does this strip tease, and out comes Bimbo La Voom or whatever the fuck they got there for names. And the guy starts singing to her. Can you beat it?" Pete drew close to Dennis, held his arms down and licked the boy's lips. "Want me to tell you what the song was, right?"

Dennis nodded.

"He sang

> Love to love you, baby,
> Loving's such delight.
> Got to love you, baby,
> Love you day and night.

And she was dancing around like a fucking yo-yo, all over the place, when he's going to all this trouble trying to set a romantic mood to the proceedings." He licked Dennis' lips again, kissed him with a slow, deep pull as Dennis squirmed, trying to free his arms.

"Struggle," Pete told him between kisses. "Be like your brother. If I had him here like this. Fight me, baby."

Everybody loves Iron Mike, Dennis thought.

"So then the guy sings

> Love to strip you baby,
> Stripping's such delight . . ."

That's what happened to Johnny, Dennis thought.

> "Got to strip you, baby,
> Strip you day and night . . ."

And this is what happens to me, Dennis thought.

"And so he just sets right in to peeling her. Boy, was it *hot* there. And the tape is rolling, like saxophones. Dirty drums. Every guy in the place is just one big hard-on and no one's saying nothing. Not a word do you hear, little brother. Not a word in the whole place. Feeling it all the way down your spine to your toes." He took up a tube of something from the floor. "Mike's little brother." He raised Dennis' legs and bent him back, almost in half. "So then he sings

> *Love to fuck you baby,*
> *Fucking's such delight . . ."*

Crooning, stroking his thighs, working him open.

> *"Got to fuck you, baby,*
> *Fuck you day and night."*

The setter slid inside Dennis with great sincerity and they moved together, first time, not a word in the whole place.

After a bit, Dennis asked, "Is it always this easy?"

"Honeybunch," said Pete, "would you be surprised."

The surprises were coming almost one a day now. Elating events were gathering about Dennis; he felt delightfully seized. There was an odd feeling of a pattern about it, as if things were being planned around him. The mail was his career, contracts and cassettes, his songs come alive, songs of masquerade designed to uphold pretty lies. Pretty lies are popular. The theatre was his magic, buying tickets to shows and seeing them whole instead of sneaking in for the second act. Some afternoons Dennis would sit on Pete Reever's stoop, waiting for him to saunter home with a beer can in his hand, and Pete would nod at Dennis with a half-smile and come up and stand where Dennis sat, and when Dennis got up Pete would whisper, "Who do you like, little brother?"

Or Dennis would sift the city, seeking song premises in the eyes he passed, content—the hypocrite! I say so myself—that no one he saw knew anything about him. Few did in the whole world. Mike did. And Dennis thought that Mike reminded him of Nora, and Nora reminded him of the Victrola, and the dancing, and the sorry lovers swaying, which is such a stupid picture to put into a song, because, look: are lovers supposed to be the only people who get to be sorry? Who gave them the monopoly? And Dennis felt, instinctively and strongly, that he would be most comfortable where nothing reminded him of anything.

The first time he walked into a gay bar—a gaudy, rectangular fire trap decorated with campy souvenirs—Dennis let an older man in a suit buy him a beer.

"So you do talk," said the man.

Dennis went home with him to see if the apartment matched the suit, and it did: the kind of apartment that is infatuated with New York, so that the hung walls and balanced free pieces seem hungry for the crowds on the street. The kind of apartment that blends the two Mets with a memory of Lindy's and Figaro's and a glimpse ahead to the next office tower of capital-owning proles hefting equipment representing power.

"Do you speak that way naturally," the man asked, "or is it a put on?"

"What way?" replied Dennis, suddenly knowing. Rich kids. A snake pit with a million snakes.

The man had a piano and Dennis played.

"Interesting," said the man. "I had thought you were a delivery boy. Of course, I mean that as a compliment."

Dennis ignored him and the man shut up and listened.

"What is that from?" the man asked.

"From me."

"Sing the words."

Dennis sang "Living in the Future," then "Dating Myself" and "Now I'm Running."

"What wonderful sad songs."

Dennis smiled in confusion. "These songs aren't sad."

"The way you sing them is sad, too."

"Listen, I'll play you a sad song." Dennis reclaimed Nora's waltz, but he broke off before he finished.

"A lovely tune."

"It's not lovely. It's antique junk."

"Funny, that's just what I feel like tonight."

A dark-haired, well-built younger man with a keen jaw came in from a bedroom, pulling on a tennis sweater. "That sounded nice," he said.

"Sad," said the suit man. "It's all so sad."

The newcomer held out his hand. "Bill Fears."

"Of course, who doesn't?" said the suit man. "But exactly what does Bill fear? Death by water? Being brutally raped? *Not* being brutally raped?"

"Were those your songs?" Bill asked Dennis.

"Yes."

"Play that one again that had the ragtime in it."

" 'Living in the Future.' "

"Listen, Ardie," the sweater man urged.

"Oh please," moaned the suit man, with a deprecating wave. "Call me when there's one about an aging bon vivant who gets a marvelous man, all his own."

"I'm not marvelous enough for you?"

"I meant for free. For love."

Dennis stopped playing. "Love isn't for free," he said. "You always pay something."

"God and Alice Faye! A teenager, and already he talks like an old queen!"

"Has this been going on all this time?" Dennis asked. "Grand pianos and white sweaters with colored stripes at the edges, and these secret jokes, all together? Or is this something new?"

Bemused, the other two stared at him.

"Because I grew up about twenty blocks south of here. My whole life. And I was watching. But nobody told me this was around."

"Fascinato," said the suit man. "I love your act. I *love* it. How would you like to play your songs for my next party?"

Bill pantomimed "yes" in mock conspiracy.

"Yes."

"Said Bill. It's five weeks from Saturday, at the Pines. You know where that is."

"Why should I?"

The suit man turned to the sweater man. "Don't you love his act? But he's too intense to be pretty."

"Go easy, Ardie," said the sweater man.

"That's what they told Alexander the Great! Napoleon! and Debra Paget! And what happened to them?"

"He doesn't get you, Ardie." The sweater man turned to Dennis. "Right?"

"You look just like my brother," said Dennis.

"And what's he?" said the suit man. "A trucker? A towel man at the Everard? Is he Spanish, with a deep navel and a Castillian lisp?"

"You don't know what you're talking about!" fired Dennis, rising from the piano. "He's an incredible guy!"

Silence.

"Well," the suit man finally said, "if your brother looks like our Bill, you're a lucky boy. Imagine having the love of a beautiful man for free."

"Give him your card, Ardie," said the sweater man. "You will play for the party, won't you?"

"Free accommodations for the weekend," said the suit man. "No fee. You pay travel."

"Ardie!"

The suit man gave Dennis a card. "Call me. We'll work it out."

"Carla Feller is recording 'Living in the Future,' " said Dennis.

"What?"

"That song you just heard. She recorded it."

"So listen, you—"

"It hasn't come out yet. Her next LP. I wrote it and she sings it."

"You have possibilities," said the suit man. "Who was your agent?"

The card read, "Ardrey. The Advisor," and gave two telephone numbers, one in New York and one in Los Angeles.

"Call me," said the suit man. "Will you call me?"

"Where have you been?" said Mike, a little sore, when Dennis came home in the late evening some days later.

"Where . . . when?"

"For the last two weeks."

It was the longest they'd been apart in their lives, Dennis suddenly realized. "It was an accident," he said.

"There's mail," said Aunt Molleen, from the kitchen. "And a wonderful great ham."

"How come it's an accident," said Mike, "that you can't call me up and come over for dinner? Huh? What're you waiting for, tickets?"

"No," said Dennis, opening a record-shaped package. "I'd second-act you for free."

"Is that supposed to be a joke?" Mike asked, his arms folded across his chest.

"Look," said Dennis, unwrapping an LP in a plain sleeve with typed labels. He extended it to Mike, but his brother's eyes refused to lower. That's how Johnny always looked, Dennis thinks. "Aunt Molleen, come see."

She would have done, then, for a magazine's nostalgia cover, the crinkly old soul wiping her hands on an apron and wondering if it was worth getting her spectacles.

"An advanced pressing," said Dennis. "I'm real."

"A pressing," said Aunt Molleen, thrilled. "And what would that be, now?"

"Carla Feller's new album. Two of my songs are on it." He found the bands. "See?"

"Thank the saints, it's a Hollywood extravaganza!"

"Iron Mike?"

Mike had turned away to gaze out the window. "Congratulations," he said, over his shoulder. "I'll leave you to celebrate."

"And me with a ham in the oven?" cried Aunt Molleen. "I'll bar the door with my bones themselves!"

Mike squared off with Dennis. "Are you going to tell me why you been making yourself scarce?"

It was simple. Dennis had been truly busy for the first time in his life: having dinner with Ardie and Bill, listening to records on Ardie's stereo, working up a new batch of songs, and sharpening his delivery for his coming debut at Ardie's party. He had been meeting people who worked at unusual hours, in the dark, and listening to them, and watching them wonder if his clothes promised some new style. Neighborhood chic.

It was simple, but Dennis saw in Mike's eyes the hope for another explanation, one simpler, less busy, with fewer people in it. "After dinner," said Dennis. "We'll talk. Okay?"

"Okay," said Mike, but he was grouchy and Dennis was distracted and dinner was dim looks penetrated by Aunt Molleen's generously dilated speculations as to whether she ought to invest her life's savings in a phonograph in order to hear Dennis' music.

Dennis said he would buy her one for the present he had offered her.

Mike said that reminded him of ma.

Aunt Molleen said if only the dear was alive to see the good fortune.

Dennis said Mike could have a present, too.

This is what Mike said: "The present I want from you is from now on you make sure you check in with me once a week, no matter what. I don't care how many records you're on or something else like that, you be there. All right?"

Dennis nodded.

After, they walked to Mike's apartment.

"Promise you won't be sore," Dennis began.

"I'll be sore if I feel like."

"The trouble is, you're going to feel like."

"Is it something I have to know?"

"It's something I have to tell."

"Why do you have to tell me, if it's going to make me sore?"

Because you're the only friend I have. Because you always stood up for me, and taught me how to carry myself like a man, and didn't hate me because I saw you when you were vulnerable. Because I love you. Go ahead and tell him.

"Because," said Dennis, "we're not kids now. We'll be living in different places and running with different people. And I'm afraid we're going to lose the chance to . . . to know each other."

"The hell you say. Running with like who different people?"

"Like with grand pianos and suits with tiny white stripes and a vest."

"Rich people? Because of your songs?"

"Yes."

"Well, so what?"

"So we ought to talk . . . before . . ."

"Look, I told you I want to hear from you once a week or—"

"You will, Iron Mike. I promise. Now listen. And if you get sore, you're going to hurt me. Know that."

"I won't hurt you, little brother."

"I'm gay."

Mike blinked at Dennis. "What does that mean?"

"You know what that means."

"Are you sure?"

"As sure as you are that you're not."

Nothing.

"How could I not be sure about what I'm attracted to?" Dennis went on. "On the street, in movies, in bars, in my mind—"

"Gay bars, you mean? Have you been going to gay bars?"

"Yes."

"And you go to bed with guys?"

Dennis paused and shrugged very slightly, keeping his face blank. Mike got up, stood around for a moment, then turned on the television.

Dennis turned it off. "Please listen."

"I hear you."

"You're getting sore."

"You're damn fucking straight I'm sore. No brother of mine is going to—"

"A brother of yours *has*! And I'm about the only brother you've got. Except for a vague connection in the aunt department, I'm your whole family. And, what's probably more important, you're mine."

Mike threw himself on the couch. "Why did you have to tell me this?"

"I wanted you to know."

"*Why,* I'm asking you?"

"Because . . . I told you . . . we have to get everything down between us . . . before—"

"This? We had to get this down, right? I guess next thing you'll tell me about your exploits. Your partners. Anyone I know? Sneaky, maybe? Or how about Father Doyle?"

"Pete Reever."

"Very funny. The Duke of Macho."

"Honeybunch, would you be surprised."

Mike looked at Dennis for a moment, then shook with sudden rage. "Don't you *ever* talk to me that way!"

They stared at each other.

"Okay," said Dennis. "Okay, I won't." He took a deep breath. "You've been mad at me all day. Maybe you could lighten up."

"*Me* lighten up?"

"What's so awful, anyway? You're not the one who's gay. I am."

"So you admit it's awful."

"No. But you think it is."

"Everyone thinks it is."

"Everyone used to think the Irish were awful."

Nothing.

"Do you want me to go? Now? And just forget you ever lived? Or am I still your brother?"

"You know damn well you're my brother."

"Well, do you still like me?"

"What the flying fuck is that a question to ask?"

"Then why do you sound so sore?"

"*Because I am sore!*" Mike roared.

"I didn't make the world. It just happened."

"Terrific. Headline news!"

"I better quit while I'm behind. Maybe after a few days you won't mind anymore." Dennis paused at the door. "Try to remember that you and I . . . you know . . ."

"No, I don't know anything tonight."

"We go back. We're invested."

129

Mike seemed to shake his head as he nodded it. "All right, Dennis. We'll talk again in a few days. Right now maybe I've heard enough out of you."

Dennis told the doorknob, "You know, I believe that's the first time in my life that you called me by my name."

Nothing.

"Okay," said Dennis. "Okay. Yeah, okay," shutting the door. Down the hall to the elevator. Then Mike comes out looking madder than before, and says, "We're not finished yet," and beckons Dennis back inside to the thrift shop furniture, junk like Nora's. Junk like his father, wounded in bed clutching the whiskey. Like Nora's waltz, that Brill Building drivel. Like Johnny, the sullen snake. A life story, up to now; there you have it. Nora's music stands out, because it was fire that, inextinguishable, had to be borne, even built. In her way, she provided Dennis with what he needed, for if she would not lend him love, she could hand him a key to his talent, make him need to use it.

"I have something to say about this," Mike said, Dennis but half hearing him. Anyway, Mike had nothing to say. What he meant was that they must shake hands in their accustomed ritual, but they reached for each other, and held on, and it occurred to Dennis that, if one will go around embracing his brothers, Johnny feels like an outline cut in stone, while Mike feels like a brother.

Now, Mike is holding Dennis tightly, because he feels him slipping away to live in the future. But Dennis is holding Mike more tightly yet, in order to bid farewell to his past with the proper respect.

Ardie's house was on the ocean near the eastern end of the Pines, choice terrain. Essentially one huge rectangular space open to the sea through sliding glass, it hid two levels of sleeping and appurtenant rooms at the two short sides, and was apparently going to contain upward of three hundred people.

"Some will arrive in plumed head dresses, as if they were Aztec executioners," Ardie remarked. "Others in rarest linens and simple totemic jewelry, like sacrificial victims." They were sitting on the seaward terrace Friday before the bash, drinking and talking as Dennis fingered the rented piano.

"There is nothing like an amazing party to keep you on the A-list. Dazzling setting, superb refreshments, and splendid guests are standard now. I give them *entertainment!*" He looked at Dennis. "Boy wonder, you're not doing your drink."

"Neat piano."

"And Bill will wear the navy blue trunks and the sheer blouse with the navy blue tie, won't you?"

"If you want, Ardie."

"And they will quietly go mental."

Footsteps along the walk, and a tough-looking woman strode in. She was the fabulous witch of PR known as The Firing Gun, after the motto of her firm: "Talent loads the gun. Publicity fires it." She asked, of Ardie, about Dennis, "This?"

"Ah," said Ardie, "if it isn't the twelve dancing princesses herself. I believe I think of you as a piñata set to mambo. Do you mind? Yes, that's boy wonder."

"Has he *signed?*"

"He hasn't. Of course, he will."

The Firing Gun approached Dennis. "Do you know who I am?"

"Don't let them subdue you, Dennis," Bill called out.

"I can *connect* you or *destroy* you."

"Hello," said Dennis.

"Why haven't you signed, you pizza waiter, you grubby complacent urchin?"

"Don't worry," Ardie assured her. "Bill wants him to sign, and he does everything Bill asks."

Not because Bill looked like Mike, but because he was sensible.

"Dennis," said Bill, "this is the Firing Gun."

She surveyed him. "I hate soft eyes. They photograph like tears."

"Lady, I'm hard," said Dennis. "Try me."

It was like that now. Suddenly, always, you spoke abruptly and with a twist, and everybody was amused.

"You know what they do to sign?" said the Firing Gun. "In

L.A.? Do you? They line up to commit acts of *unspeakable* corruption. *To be noticed!*"

Dennis ran through a bit of "Dating Myself."

"Carla Feller's people got him to sign a great deal away prematurely," Bill explained. "He's being cautious."

"Interesting," said Ardie. "Carla Feller's people are our people."

Bill nodded. "There is only one PR."

"Let's hear him sing."

Smiling, Dennis filled in a few lines of the song.

"Rustic," pronounced the Firing Gun. "Beat. Eclectic."

"Firing," said Bill, "is that a rave or what?"

She took Bill by the hand and stroked the hair on his arm momentarily. "Do you know what I hate? Do you? Dark men."

Dennis knew he would sign and so did Ardie. They settled their business just before the party got going, at about eleven o'clock Saturday night, at the piano. "You'll get something really nice for this," Ardie told him. "Then you and I will make a lot of money. Would you like a house like this one?"

And guests like Ardie's?—including a number of international celebrities who had done nothing in their lives but spend money; three TV hunks (eighteen counting daytime) who threw cover to the winds and went for each other on sight; and theatre people, noticeably quiet, their talent cowed by others' cheap fame; and music people, so enlightened by drugs of pleasure they were walking through walls; and fashion people, who paid Ardie dearly in some coin or other to be there; and houseboys, agents, terse pimps, independent filmmakers, defunct poets, capering paparazzi, rigid heirs, uncouth entrepreneurs, arrogant waiters, servile expressionistic cartoonists, self-propelled oblivious pin-headed interviewers . . . the catalogue of contempo socì. Dennis stayed sober till he went on, well after two, and, in the middle of "Dating Myself," Carla Feller pushed through the crowd and took over the tune as Dennis laid out and gave her more and more piano, and they hotted it up together, till at the end he leaned across the piano to shake her hand on the last beat as the crowd let out choice yells and a hundred cameras went off. Ardie and the Firing Gun exchanged nods.

The party was so crowded that every so often bouncers passed through to throw out insignificant others and those who, in those first years of the Higher Substance Abuse, had not yet learned how to hold their combinations. Breathing and motion were further hampered by the antics of those trying to become items of gossip, and by the celebs, packed up in their entourages and threading paths through the crowd, as ornate and slow as Venetian funerals.

Finally Dennis walked down to the water for some air, and stood on the wet sand in white cotton trousers and a black silk shirt looking for the moon.

"What an amazing stunt that was with Carla Feller," said Bill, coming up out of the darkness with his tennis sweater draped around his shoulders. "Who staged that?"

"No one."

"Someone. They just didn't let you in on it. Carla Feller doesn't hit middle C without Randy Newman writing the charts, Bob Mackie building her gown, Ron Field teaching her dance, and a hundred fans filling in the clap track. I imagine the Firing Gun set that one up. Who else can calculate that kind of spontaneity?"

"She says she'll make me a cover line inside of a year," said Dennis. "What's that mean?"

"The blurbs on magazine covers."

"She told me my voice is acid but acid voices are A-list this year."

Bill touched Dennis' shoulder, a friendly touch, undemanding. The touch of a straight man. "What's your brother like?" he asked. "The one I remind you of."

"He's . . . he's very admirable. Kind of a lunkhead, and sort of tough at the edges. But very nice. They call him Iron Mike. He taught me how to whistle."

"He sounds hot."

"Someone like Ardie would say he's going to waste it. He'll pledge himself to a wife and children, the sooner the better."

Bill sighed quietly, almost happily. "What sort of woman does an Iron Mike marry? His mother?"

Clouds raced over the black beach.

Dennis said, "When last heard from, he was mixed up with someone intelligent and beautiful and ambitious. A college type. It was two things at once, really, because you could tell she was a little afraid of him and at the same time he dazzled her. But what she feared was what dazzled, you know? It's the kind of thing songwriters love to work with, because it puts a little . . . a little bite on the sweet tunes. You know, like, 'I'm afraid without you but I'm also afraid of you.' And he could be tough with her if he wanted to. But instead he's very kind. And that's devastating. I know it is. I know it. And she can't get that from those Harvard guys, because the only reason they're kind is because they're *not* tough. You know? Iron Mike is kind because he isn't afraid. And I bet there's this great shortage of nice, admirable men, and she knows it. She's holding off from him right now, but that won't last long. He's too wonderful to resist. So she's going to jilt all the Harvard guys and go for Iron Mike. It's what we call marrying out of the neighborhood."

"That's a rather gay notion, isn't it?" said Bill, scooping up a handful of sand and letting it run through his fingers. "The mating of princess and peasant. An idyll by E. M. Forster, maybe. 'The Articled Clerk and the Bulging Sailor.' "

Dennis missed the allusion, but caught the concept. "Listen, there are times when a peasant is a prince. Don't you know that they're stolen in infancy by pirates?" Dennis whistled, a baroque chitter in falling minor thirds. "That means 'Come out, all clear.' To Mark Revien, anyway."

Bill looked back at the Pines skyline, dotted with lights and humming with rumor. "Speaking of pirates. . . ." he said. Dennis looked, too: at the marvelous shacks where the aesthetes have the money and beauty is a toy.

"If Iron Mike saw me at this party," Dennis said, "he'd probably belt me."

"He sounds wonderful."

These Pines dos have a way of giving out quite suddenly, for no one wants to be the last to leave. They may swell all night, but they can thin to a host and his devotees in a moment. Not long after dawn, Dennis nodded awake in a chair and found the great room empty and denuded of courtiers. Even the servants had gone. No, not empty—the Firing Gun was checking through some papers on the couch and Ardie, at the piano, was polishing off a cigarette of occult manufacture, held between thumb and pinkie. Bill came in from the terrace, naked.

"Hasn't he?" Ardie asked the Firing Gun. "Done well?"

"The bit with Carla came off *beautifully*. Formal. Organic. Holistic."

"He has," Ardie answered his question.

Dennis shook himself awake.

"Come see," said Ardie, leading Bill toward Dennis. "Is he not primo? So many of the men you buy are lurid punks, like a hard-rock version of love. But see how aristocratically this man is built. Even his bulk is sleek." Ardie kneaded Bill's shoulder muscles. "The pecs are curious and knowledgeable, with their dust of hair. The dark thighs, a melody of power. The hard stomach. The hands are gentle but the arms are forceful. The eyes never leave you. He's a dreamboat. He was born for pleasure. He's a prince of love."

Dennis glanced at the Firing Gun; she sipped a Kahlua and milk. "So?" she said.

Bill, smiling, took Dennis by the hand and led him upstairs.

"I told you you'd get something nice," said Ardie, as they went.

The sun was up. As he pulled the blinds to, Bill said, "What would you like to do, Dennis?"

"I'd like to show you the new position all the hotshots love."

"That's for me."

"Get on your back."

Bill tilted his head and rubbed his brow. "Well . . . I don't usually catch."

"You don't have a thing to worry about, because I'm going to be real nice to you. A fellow taught me and now I'll teach you. It's real sincere. See, you toss your secrets down the airshaft where no one'll find them and then you honeybunch a guy till he is content. A toke helps, but is not necessary. Not in Tara."

Bill looked at Dennis as if he feared the boy would pull out a knife, but Dennis laughed and shrugged, and they petted each other and fell into bed and forgot the world as good buddies should.

Downstairs, Ardie went over the Carla Feller PR printouts to see where Dennis might fit in.

In Manhattan, Aunt Molleen was having the day's second cup of tea. Mike had just left for work; he still kissed her at the door.

Pete Reever, nude, was staring out his window at an earnest young man in the bottom half of a Brooks Brothers suit and a striped shirt, tying a brown tie. Pete very slowly began to move his hips, grinning.

Sneaky Pazillo was awake in bed, imagining himself being chased through the Pentagon by a squad of five-star generals to the strains of "The Syncopated Clock."

Charlene Bono, who had taken an early vacation from the office, was trying out a new fashion makeup combo kit and pondering whether to succumb to or resist the blandishments of her current beau, the tender but insistent Moose Laferriere. She wondered why men were always trying to get you into bed.

Father Doyle was masturbating, thinking of Jackie Onassis.

And the Scornful Witch of Fooley, still determined to bring down the House of Tara—because it's there—was setting out the chess pieces for a last game with the King, winner take all.

PART THREE

The Reigns of the Princes in the Kingdom of Tara

Who owns Dublin Johnny Keogh, the King of Tara? What are his themes? He came into his kingdom a lover, not a leader; and not loyal but reckless. The Scornful Witch of Fooley did well to teach him that fatal charm of romance, for she carefully neglected to warn him what stalks the insatiable romantic: improvidence and degradation. One's health dissolves as whiskey eats the blood, as folly shatters the soul, as God looks on. So the King collected his harem, lived for a kind of love, a taking kind. He gave pleasure, never peace. He was born ambitious, an oaf of the counties chosen to come to the city, to wander and then settle, planting his banners and ordering his kind, his tribe, his sons. See the choices he made, then, the dismay he wrought. The Witch owned him, and he owned nothing.

The rogue. In dotage before a fair time, his energy sagging like his belly, he would still turn toward beauty, still delight in the fear he could inspire, claim his power. He fell. His theme was love, but a lover builds generosity, nurture, tenderness. Pure passion, passion alone, is theft, corruption, a violence. The greedy lord of the secrets. His theme. His kind. His city truth, swirling down from the soaring monster buildings of the rich and devious into the mean places of the working people. Scavenger king. The Witch knew her man. The Witch. Who knew her themes, why she pursues one and not another, why she dishonors Tara, her own land, why she fails to destroy the connectors who pop up here and there, always in alignment to introduce, and to inspire, and to preserve? Mayhap this failure to surround her enemies attests to her sense of humor. It is said that she smiled as she played her chess with the King of Tara, grinned as his queen was thwarted and laughed at every toppling of bishop and knight.

One evening, she toured all Tara at a go, flying from part to part, sure of her work. There was Dublin Johnny at the door of a liquor store in Forest Hills late on a Saturday, his eyes roving the street through the glass as Johnny presented the mouth of his gun to the head of the proprietor, urging him to disburse the day's take or court a penalty. Just walk in and ask, the family motto. The Witch compared Dublin Johnny's tired gaze with the infatuated belligerence in Johnny's eyes, and knew, as she had long known, that wickedness, too, has feelings. Exhaustion and war: the themes.

Bare moments later, the Witch noted Mike strolling Third Avenue with Erica, and disliked their warmth. There she had failed, thinking the man a simpleton who would ruin his hopes with coarse practices, the woman a fearful bigot. Whence his kindness, her daring? But then he was not truly a Keogh, was he?—his adulterous conception had not been looked for. Some other strain had gifted him with the ability to befriend a woman, throwing off all actuarial judgment calls on the future of Tara. As for her, his little princess, some Jews are unpredictable, and especially baffling to the Irish, even to an Irish witch. They have a wisdom of kind that has defied the centuries. That day on the street after the three-month separation, the Witch watched Erica shyly promenading up to Mike, watched him still and uncertain, watched her quicken the pace and smile, watched him hold out his arms like a father crouching at the edge of the schoolyard, watched her run to him like a child set free. The Witch shook her head at this. Lovely sex she knows, but sexual love irritates her.

Later and last, the Witch looked in on Dennis, scribbling in his notebook. The Witch knew Dennis best of all and felt most dear about him, for he alone could wither the confidence of the impervious Mike, and then the ruin of Tara would be thorough. How close are brothers? They are most close when the parents are most distant. How true is kind? Kind is truest when alien ways are most threatening. How mean are secrets, how fatal? The Witch knows one to dismay Mike, and Dennis can tell it. How good are intentions when the war is on?

Let us see how it goes with Tara.

Exhaustion and war, Dublin Johnny and his son, were partners. But war trades in youth and speed, and Dublin Johnny was failing now, bleeding from many wounds. One he took in a raid on a mom-and-pop grocery, for mom surprised with bite. One he felt in the dissolution of his family, for though he wove no pattern for affection himself, surely in the end he wished for something of the like to pull up around him in the cold. "Bad work," he called it. "Worrying the heart out of a man. Bad work, Johnny." At least he had his one son, his oldest. But for him, Dublin Johnny might have caved in long since.

When not fostering his da and moving in with and out on various daughters of joy, Johnny held informal court in a bar named The Labyrinth. Few waited on him, true enough, for his fierce countenance betokened no likely camaraderie. But it was there one met the necessary connectors in Johnny's line of work.

Johnny had come to The Labyrinth to find a new partner—or, no, that's like saying he needed a new da. Johnny wants a bravo, a henchman. Trying to remember what a sardonically welcoming smile looked like—really, just trying his best to smile—Johnny glanced about him to see what suite might accommodate him. A few idle conversations led at length to an expressively average man with a fast grin and slightly humble eyes, amiable and quickly cowed, the kind who could provoke a thousand conflicting descriptions from eyewitnesses. The secret of The Life, Johnny had learned, was to work with men who were neither forceful nor flabby, not winners but not yet dismayed, either. Johnny took the reins; that was his ride. All he could use was a spotter riding shotgun. A smallish guy, just enough anxious about Johnny's size to defer invariably to him. An able schmo. He found one.

"Will I see them again?" Dublin Johnny muttered. Sometimes he spoke in his sleep in the darkness, and Johnny listened. "Who will I see?"

Johnny waited for the breathing rhythm. None. He came over to the bed. "Da?"

"Who will be there for me?"

Johnny shook him.

"Who are you pushing at, damn you?"

"You're awake." Johnny clasped his da's hands. "So."

"So."

"Shall I fetch Dennis again?"

"To a hell with it, Johnny! And all of them, all in it, all along!" His body shook with coughing, and his right fist shot forth, once, twice, somewhat in the manner of the young Dublin Johnny, having what he wanted. "To a hell with it, now. Why now, eh? Johnny? Dennis . . ."

". . . and the other one?"

They looked at each other. Dublin Johnny broke first, with a hoarse grunt. The weeping miscreant, once expert in a minor art and now good for nothing. His kingdom in ruins. "Ah, what is more unfashionable," said Dublin Johnny, "than an old man?"

Johnny had to leave, to meet his schmo, to do his work. The act is simple, the calculation a routine, the choosing of the target the sole hazard. Seek harmless places, modest people easily overwhelmed by the pointed exactions of Johnny Keogh. "Don't make it bad work, Johnny," his da reminds him as the boy departs, Great American Johnny in the dark at the door, as it closes, and Johnny cannot look back. "Don't make it bad work," Dublin Johnny pleads, alone. "The echo of it," he goes on, "will follow you on forever."

Johnny answers his calling well, but the pay is chicken feed for the risk. One day he'll walk into a police stake-out, and that will be bad work, sure. The schmo and he split the take and separate, the schmo on foot and Johnny in his car. He does not want to go home, and visits The Labyrinth to see what there is, on all earth, for our lifetimes. Yes, there are such moments of conclusive survey, especially after a night like this one of Johnny's, with his da prattling of lost people when it was himself threw them away, and Johnny's gun paying him off in pennies and the acquaintance of schmos, and his girls a cold portion all told, except for the pleasure of the bed—and all this bound up in the realization that this night is like all others. That Johnny's life is all a prattling da and schmos.

Standing at the bar of The Labyrinth, Johnny felt the whispers come upon him. He shuddered them off by turning his ear to the talk around him.

"Some broad I got me," one man was telling a companion.

"She don't own you, does she? Does she own you?"

"All week she wants to go here, go there." His head wagged in imitation, but the voice remained his. "Buy me this. Take me to such a movie. Can my girlfriend come?"

"Her girlfriend."

"Believe it."

"And her girlfriend's dog, how about? A poodle, maybe."

"Comes the weekend, *please,* she's too tired."

"Never fails."

Johnny watched them heft their beers. He imagined the women these men had, shaggy fat bozos that they are. What woman could get anything from guys like them except proof that any company isn't better than no company?

"Think they've got this deal going, see?" the first man went on. "Real neat deal. I get to plug her, and she gets to bill me. Restaurant this, movie that." The head again. "So much plug, so much money spent in return."

"So how neat is it?"

"It's pretty neat. Long as she don't find somebody she can bill bigger than me. That day comes, it's Sayonara. No, she don't own me. And I don't own her. It's like a . . ."

A business partnership, Johnny thought.

". . . a maid."

"She could do the dishes in one of those la-di-da aprons and nothing else, right? Then you could sit behind her and watch her fanny dance."

"That's a fucking good idea."

"Let's drink to it."

Johnny thought of his women and their deals. He had never viewed it so, yet the analysis was persuasive. I give so much, they give so much. A trade, keeping score. This perhaps explained why some of them would weep in bed as he lay with them. The nicer ones. Weeping because the deal favors the man: the one who holds.

"Bet she wants you to marry her," said the second guy.

"No."

"No?"

"She don't say she does." He looked perplexed, wondering whether this new idea implied a dishonor.

"Maybe she's waiting for the right time."

"Maybe."

"She'll hit you for it one of these days. You can always count on a broad that way."

"I can't count on *nobody.*"

"That's also true."

"Maybe get out of the city, you know? Try the suburbs. Too much activating around here."

"So what's the suburbs? Shopping centers and community colleges."

"Yeah, but everybody's head is quiet, see? That's what I like. There's no one gawking around at something they want that you got. Everybody's got a lawn with grass, everybody's got a water hose. No one's looking for anything, got it?"

"So let's drink to it."

"So let's."

Johnny left The Labyrinth and drove to Manhattan. To the

144

neighborhood. To the park at the river where he used to whisper, a melancholy clearing in the stone wood. The baglady was waiting for him.

"The crop of a busted family," quoth she, "is despair. How is it holding up, boy? What do you miss?" She rustled her baggage, checking, looking. "Time passes, and we stand still." She pulled out some papers. "Good wind up tonight. Dead leaves whipping by you. Once they were green, now they're junk. That's life, boy. A mess that someone else gets to clean up when the wind blows us away. It's all here, at last." She rattled her papers. "Writing my stories down. Got to tell what I been seeing. Want to hear? It's hotter than *Coronet.*"

Johnny shook his head.

"Want to kiss me cute?"

Johnny looked at her.

"You're still a baby, I know that. Sad-looking boy. The best kind, if you ask me. I know about it. We all need a friend. Sometimes a stranger is as close as you get." She fussed at her papers. "This is a story about stray dogs. You're in it."

Johnny grabbed at the papers and tossed them in the air. The breeze took them spinning up the street.

"Sure, tell me how you feel about it. You ought to go on the fights, fierce boy like you. Man of action. I see you, sure. Look at how tall. They'd be cheering. The money is good. Cheer for that look in your eye, tender. Call you a name, think about it. Kid Danger, that's you. Got to look out for the exploitation, though. Managers. Lot of corruption up at the top. You do the fighting, they get the money. You know it. You know it." She laughed. "You look so tough, don't you? Oh, but I see what else is in it. See the pain. Everyone hurts you, right. You hurt back. It's good. How many girls you hurt, tender? I need to know for my next story."

Johnny got up.

"Kid Danger. Why don't you run your own fights? Call it Kid Danger's Saturday Special. Amateur slugging contests."

Like Steel Fist.

"Let them fight, and you get the money."

She has something there. Anyone can hire an arena, print posters, collect a staff, pay off the blues. And Johnny knew he could get up something better than Steel Fist. Hell, who couldn't? A little coaching. A little PR. A little show biz.

"Kid Danger's Saturday Special." She gave a start and stared at the sky. "Somebody's dying. I can always tell. Someone we know."

His da is dying.

"Right now. Can you feel it, boy?"

Why go on knocking off two-bit cash boxes when you can go big without the risk?

"He's calling for a friend. Only animals want to die alone." She listened. "What's he saying? Hear him? What's he want? It's dark. He thought he was sleeping. She's with him. Likes to be there at the end. What's he saying to her?"

Aroused, interested in something for the first time in years, Johnny walked off to his car.

"He's saying, 'Let me see you.' That's what he says. 'Let me see you.'"

Across the river in Brooklyn, she revealed herself to him, and Dublin Johnny saw her and fell back on the bed, checkmate, and the King of Tara was no more.

In the years in which Johnny pursued the furtive anarchy of the small-time bandit, Mike hefted himself up through the ranks of his union, setting and bolting. Then, back on earth, he directed the shakeout and the pick, when the beams and columns are dropped off, sorted out, and sent topside on the ball, tied in the two choker cables.

Ironworkers do not get ahead by exceeding the received pace or setting the steel in a state of grace: ironworkers do not get ahead, period. Anyway, the job itself, by the nature of its unique breakdown into two-man teams, calls for an immaculately balanced expertise, a perfect competence. Slacking or showboating would throw the balance out, maybe fatally. Mike caught onto this at once, and made utter reliability his trademark. His foremen liked him, and always called for him when they were getting up teams for the next job. He was learning more than the balance of high iron, for men in other unions would seek him out for lunch-break talks in the bashful homage that the aficionado pays the torero. Mike took the advantage offered, and asked them about their work, for he had decided to march through the trade and become a building contractor himself.

It was worth remarking that, while almost every task in the raising of a building calls for specialty of craft, not every worker could articulate the elation of skill he brought to what he did; and not every worker seemed to care all that much that he *could* do a thing many others in the world could not. The different unions, too, seemed to attract different kinds of men, none of them rivalling the powerhouse dash of the ironworker. Local 28, the sheet metal workers, were the most pacific; Local 20, the cement finishers, the most rowdy; and Local 46, the lathers, the most pretentious, maneuvering their reinforcement bars into the concrete as if they were surgeons granting life to a troubled organism and ceaselessly contending with the carpenters as to which of their two unions held first rights to the fitting of plasterboard partitions.

Though Mike's intercourse with all these men was vital, in a very personal and unambitious way he loved the buildings most when they were still skeletons straining upward, before the cement finishers poured the floors for the other unions to tread upon, when the site belonged entirely to the ironworkers: because then it was pure building, the achievement of power without the decorative rhetoric, without the embellishments that render a building easier to inhabit but less joyful to admire.

"Good work cheers a man," Uncle Flaherty observed, on one of his many visits to Mike's sites. Mike was on his fourth job now, with scarcely a layoff between, and already the site was bustling with men and equipment, cranes hoisting the siding pieces into the curtain wall; expeditors hurtling from one adventure to another, now soothing a flurried electrician, then firing an overparted steamfitter; water sloshing off finished floors below as the cement was being poured onto the newer floors above; and everywhere whistles, shouts, mechanical humming, and crashes. Turn straight up and see, in the brilliance of the welding fire, a lone, empty bag of snack blow down through the air, flipping now so, now so, as the wind takes it, without a hope in its fate but to reach the street and fall under the shoes of pedestrians. Uncle Flaherty always wore his old hat, one of the outdated yellow ones without a proper side fitting. The old timers seemed to rejoice in hardship. One of the older setters invariably went shirtless when the temperature rose above fifty-five degrees.

"This is the best time of it," said Uncle Flaherty. "When the different crafts combine, each in his way but all to the one end. It's like threading a building together, Mike, my boy, making a tapestry of it, as you might say."

They were at dinner, in one of the same bent-fork joints the ironworkers' union has dined on since its formation, just after the turn of the century.

"This is the people of the land, Mike. The men who pay the taxes and fight the wars, and the women who bear their children and keep their homes and bury them. This is the country, Mike. Not the newspaper tyrants or the bums on the relief, or the movie actors or the people you'll see reading out the news on television. We are the spirit of all, Mike. Add in the farmers and the factory people and that's the whole of it, I'm telling you. And all the different kinds getting along together. In a building, Mike. On the site, I mean, the locals side by side on all the floors."

This is not entirely true, Mike thought. The ironworkers' union will not accept blacks, for one instance. Certain unions don't speak readily to certain other unions, for another, with the memory of which behaved in what ways in strikes long past.

"Should all the different kinds get along in the first place?" Mike said.

"What are you asking?"

"Even your own kind doesn't always get along. The worst fights I've seen are always two Irish guys going at it. And look at us. Our family. We're no model of getting along."

"What are you asking, I'm telling you, Mike?"

"I'm *saying*. Maybe people aren't meant to get along. No matter what kind."

"A sorry thing to hear from the son of Nora Flaherty, my own niece."

"I got news about Farrell."

"Yo?"

"Looks good. I have an interview next Wednesday in the shop. What do you think, should I dress up, like?"

Uncle Flaherty thought it about, shrugged, thought more.

"I got that suit with the vest that little brother picked out."

"A vest, Mike? In a steel and iron shop?"

Mike smiled. "The ladies seem to like it."

"Miss Erica," said Uncle Flaherty.

"How about Miss Erica among others?"

"I don't know, lad. Not a suit, sure, but not work clothes, either. Something between, then."

"Nothing's between."

"Farrell," said Uncle Flaherty. "The Farrell outfit. I worked on that First Avenue job for them. Forty-sixth Street. Back when the neighborhood was still . . . coming up in the world, ain't we all?"

"Like a column chalked up in the pick."

They both laughed.

"It's good work," said Uncle Flaherty.

Mike was up for a position with a firm dealing in structural and interior alterations in smallish buildings. The formal name of this work, seldom invoked, is miscellaneous and ornamental steel and iron work. The real name is steel and iron. The job, which involved leaving the ironworkers to run small sites himself, made him a kind of managerial punk, but it was a position full of promise. In the end, he showed up at Farrell's in the white shirt with blue stripes that Dennis had forced on him, topped off by a blue tie. The meeting went well, a man-to-man sizing up in trade lingo, and after a half hour he was hired.

This was great news, and Mike shared it by phone with Erica, Uncle Flaherty, and Aunt Molleen, those three and no others. This was the outline of Mike's sociability at the time, a strangely limited one for an attractive boy of twenty-two who made friends easily. We must note as well the omissions in the family circle, as Tara continues to dissolve in the vulgar mist of modern times. But perhaps Mike was born to found his own kingdom, one of new allegiances entirely. Yet why did he not run to Erica's for dinner with one of those little bottles of champagne for a drink to shared sympathies? Why are two people so rigorously attached not married, moreover?

This is why: directly he finished his phoning about, Mike changed out of his interview duds and sauntered over to a bar he frequented on Third Avenue, named The Dizzy Duck but known to Mike, in his moments of whimsical frolic, by a punning variation indicative of the bar's array of available women. We must not hold this a bitter reproach of a fine young man, nor take it as the lusty misapprehension of youth. Love fidelity in the absolute is one of society's most impossible propositions, one subscribed to only by those with a lack of opportunity. Erica, Mike holds, is for family, affection, support: the princess of the kingdom, to be married and swept off to the castle in due course. For now, Mike is in his prime, and must sample the world of beckoning beauty. In moderation, this sampling may invigorate, just as, in obsession, it must ruin. Those of you, my readers, who believe that matrimonial sex is the one true sensuality will have to take Mike as a flawed man; but what would you say, then, to learn that sweet Aunt Molleen loved nothing as much as to be overchanged at the grocery? Her sharp eyes counting the silver, she would, on those rare occasions when a stray nickel or quarter came into her palm, thrust the coins into her purse in a flash, and gloat over her windfall all the way home.

At The Dizzy Duck, Mike wasted little time in scouting and preamble; he knows what he likes and he has his lines down cold. He feels that he can tell what a woman needs to hear just from the way she tells him her name. Surely this is overreaching. Like half the men in the world, Mike thinks he scores better than he does —the other half think they score worse. He also thinks he has heard everything, but here's a woman to surprise him with her speed. "I always know a good man," she says, "by the number of beers he buys. A guy who thinks he can catch you in two pops is no Clark Gable, anyway."

"How many does it take, dearheart?" Mike asked.

She copped a good look at him. "Let's go," she said.

Later, she told him, "If it's all the same to you, fuck me till blood runs down my leg."

Mike was glad. This way he could like her a little more tonight and a lot less tomorrow.

Naturally, he never spoke of these exploits to Erica, and naturally she knew of them. There are three kinds of people you can never fool: your lover, your siblings, and your children. A family is an encyclopedia of your failings. Oh yes, the odd secret will keep here and there, even extraordinary ones. But your princess will gauge the extent of your love life by the very look in your eyes as you come through the door. And Erica is smart enough to know that a good man is worth forgiving one bad habit. In a way, it made him more interesting, most manly because untamable. If Erica had wanted a chaste package of a husband ready for the shelf, she knew where to get plenty. She wanted Mike.

They had never mentioned marriage except vaguely, philosophically. Quizzed by her family as to the precise status of the . . . engagement—they pronounced the ellipsis with exquisite condescension—she mildly replied, "You know as much about it as I do." They were livid and silent.

Of course, there is a trap in matches of this kind. If the woman will accept a barbarous alliance, marriage according to manly whim, without contract, it may prove not the temporary but the ultimate arrangement. But Mike is for marriage, and Erica knows it. He is young, she thinks, too young; and he has always been: but he is true. True in the long run, no matter how false at certain moments. How many husbands, to the despair of twenty million suburban wives, have proved only intermittently true, definitively false? One day Mike will turn around and, falsely cool to hide his wonder, say they shall marry. Already, he has begun to glance at it as they talk, still philosophically—or no, from the side, as if taking a look at the people in the house next door. But Erica senses an edge of personal naturalism in those glances.

"I only want girls," he said on the street one day, as they watched a couple with a child on each free hand and a third pushing her own stroller with an air of most intrepid concentration.

"Why only girls?" Erica asked. "No Parnell Junior?"

"Boys are dangerous. They disappoint you sometimes. If they're not . . ."

"What? Not what?"

"Not strong. Not successful. Girls don't have to be strong or successful."

"What do they have to be? Pretty?"

Mike smiled. "You're pretty."

"That's not an answer."

"You'll have pretty girls."

"Or that. You never know, anyway. What you'll get." Then she added, the way he would, "Huh?"

He looked at her for a while, rather a long while all told. "How could we miss?" He touched her without touching, one of his sincerest tricks, almost made her back away.

"Well," she said. "I'll bet you're one son who didn't disappoint anyone, anyway."

They walked on, and Mike thought that over. Not ma, surely, nor Uncle Flaherty nor Aunt Molleen. Da and Johnny didn't count. And Dennis, that ungrateful little fucker, was in no position to talk about who disappointed whom.

Of all Dublin Johnny Keogh's sons, Dennis came into his destiny most quickly and least boldly. When Johnny and Mike had yet to advance their professional projects, Dennis was already established. The boy knew he had left the neighborhood the night he and Carla Feller were officially introduced to contempo socì at Firbank's a few months after Ardie's Pines party, when the clerisy of the true New York town—which is to say, the media people— returned from the beaches and festivals and symposia to defy the lingering September heat and get the season going.

The reason Dennis was to be coupled with Carla Feller was that

Carla Feller was a lesbian in a business that does not tolerate exotic love modes in its mellow balladeers. As a punk rocker or blues stylist, she might have polished her image with a rumor of scandal; going over the top is virtually a convention of those genres. However, Carla sang smokey-joe MOR, and needed a flirty girlfriend image. But she didn't like men. Whose girlfriend could she be? Her first words to Dennis, when they met at the big do at Firbank's, were, "If you try to fuck me, I'll kill you." Her next words were, "The honeysweet thrill of it all!" as stooges rushed up and flashbulbs sparkled around them.

"Cut and print," said Bill.

"Den," said Carla, looking at Bill, "who on earth is this horrible testy male bimbo?" And she pranced off, followed by the press.

Dennis looked at Bill.

"When Ardie took her up," Bill explained, "he assigned me to her."

"As what?"

"As lover. That was before she discovered Sappho."

"What was *that* like?"

"Like dating Godzilla. Though in bed she gets rather Rotarian. Almost serene. Maybe she can only open up to a woman."

"What do they do, anyway? Lesbians? What can they do?"

"Don't go ghetto on me, Dennis. They do what you do, just differently." He touched Dennis' shoulder. "Okay?"

"You know, the more I hear you, the more you seem like my brother. Yet you're nothing like him, really. You're not even a . . . like a collegiate version of him. What are you?"

"She's on the floor," The Firing Gun cut in—sudden materializations were among her unique tricks. "There's a man with her. Dance with them and he'll melt away. It's *set* and it's *neat.*"

"It's city life," said Bill. "Make the arrangements. Live smart."

The Firing Gun pushed Dennis at the dance floor. "Boogie for your life," she ordered, as he left. She eyed Bill darkly. "You *hunks* expect to get away with anything."

Bill could do a superb John Wayne imitation; he did it now. "Firing, there's a train leaves town at six tonight. Be under it."

"Decadent!" she cried as she stormed off. "Feeble. Fameless."

The reason Dennis knew he had left the neighborhood was that, in his new world, all the imperatives were the opposite of those he had been raised on. In the neighborhood, everything was families and hard labor for subsistence incomes in plain English without r's: the neighbahood. Now, everybody was single and the work was service-industry software and you never knew what someone wasn't saying when he said it and everything happened at night around people who had money to kill with. Knowing he was culturally short of the mark, Dennis stuck close to Bill, for while they were not of kind, they had a sympathy going, fit companions. Sometimes they tried to be true lovers; that didn't always work. But the support did, and between men that can matter more. Anyway, Dennis had the odd feeling that Bill, for all his style, was straight. One who chose his opportunities with a certain creative tact, yes. Still. Something about Bill seemed less like the men who were filing into Dennis' new life and more like men he had known in days past. And in the mad cafés that Ardie's set frequented, they would run into smashing women who clearly regarded themselves as episodes in Bill Fears' past. Just the way they touched Bill's hand told Dennis Bill had known them absolutely.

"What are you attracted to?" Dennis asked. "Really?"

"Leisure and paid bills."

How far from the neighborhood could one go? Dennis was working, though not in any way they used to value on Second Avenue: rising in the late morning to dally over the coffee like a landlord in satin breeches—at that, not always in his rightful home at Aunt Molleen's—and ponder the available universals for a lyric hook. The profits were hand over fist, and that much impressed Aunt Molleen. But she began to comment on how unlike Dennis his songs seemed. "Who wrote those words?" she kept saying, when he'd play them over, though she knew well who.

"I'm only trying to make a hit," he'd tell her.

"Listening to you," she once said, "you'd think the whole world was a full mug of beer and a carriage to ride you around day and night."

Nor was she happy to witness Dennis' progress through the

great world as the juvenile of The Firing Gun's PR musical comedy starring Carla Feller. The day he turned up on page seven of the *New York Post*, Aunt Molleen uttered, instead of the expected trilling rhapsody, nothing.

"You always liked that stuff before," Dennis told her.

"Not with you in it."

Oddest of all, she was serene when Dennis proposed to follow Mike's trail and get his own place. Dennis had felt guilty about moving out on her after all she had done for him; now he felt something not unlike neglected.

"It's been a busy life, Dennis my boy," she told him. "What with watching out for your ma now and again, and all the guests there were in the old house as was, and your da and all the scuffles. Maybe it's time for me to keep to myself. Maybe it is, now."

Mike would give her a hug, Dennis thought, and talk her out of it or something. Mike always finds the way out for everybody. Except with Erica—I did that. And what did I get for it? A grumpy brother.

"How old are you now, Dennis?"

"Nineteen."

"Well, it'll be nearly that many years before, that I brought you into Johnny's room. He was in one of his fits and mad at the world, and I let him hold you. How it soothed him, the poor boy. No one could love him, and that's the truth of it. Even those that tried. But he was your friend, wasn't he? Once?"

Dennis nodded, wondering if she would cry.

"You'll not be taking this the wrong way, Dennis. But the peculiar developments of the Keoghs wasn't what I bargained for at the start of it all."

"You and me both," said Dennis, knowing that the hugging moment had come but resenting the urge to have to do what Mike does.

Aunt Molleen went to see about another cup of tea. "You and Mike and his foreign princess can come for dinner. And you will send me all the records of your songs, even if they do sound like opera sometimes. And it's right for you to have your own place.

But if you don't mind me butting my nose, you shouldn't be in the *New York Post*. The only Irishmen who should get their names in the newspapers is mayors and policemen shot in the line of duty."

You be good or else, Dennis thought.

Everyone was bearing down on him. Carla phoned with notions for songs and how to photograph smartly; Ardie and The Firing Gun battered him with career plotting; Bill hasseled him with moral catechisms. There were legal people, publishing people, record people, colleagues, bodyguards, drivers, liaison teams. Dennis put off moving, but Ardie pressed him, said he needed style; and Aunt Molleen took up examining *The Times* realty ads with a fierce eye.

Then there was Mike: distracted by work, protective of his romance, insistent upon and then irate at Dennis' confessions.

"If you don't like my answers," Dennis told him, "why ask the questions?" But Mike would only gorge on more questions and get even angrier. What do you do in bed? What about the drugs? Poisons pouring into America's bloodstream—*you* lead them in! What about the incurable venereal diseases, child pornography?

It's twelve midnight: do we know where Dennis' mouth is? Slurping on some nut's boner, which he just pulled out of the ass of some other nut. Then that bratty kid comes to Aunt Molleen's and kisses her, and she kisses the rest of the world. Us. Me. Then, like, it goes on, because Dennis kisses the creeping dyke Carla Feller that he's supposed to be dating and some photographer's there aiming right for her fucking tips which show right through her blouse and all America thinks, oh, that's disco just right; and if it turns out that everyone in the disco is a faggot and everyone in Hollywood's a faggot and most of New York is faggots slurping boners and smacking junk up their nose, so maybe they should develop trick cameras that only pick up boner-coking faggots so they can wipe the rest of us right off the world.

Mike was inexhaustible. He was Saint Patrick spotting his first snake. He made Dennis take him to a bar. Dennis chose the Eagle, on Twenty-first and Eleventh, because he thought the aggressively masculine atmosphere that the bike-and-western scene cultivated would reassure Mike.

They had scarcely popped their beers when Mike, taking in the preponderance of leather costume, not only jackets but pants and caps and even shirts, muttered, "What is this supposed to be, a Nazi folk dance?"

Then Dennis, on his way back from the men's room, spotted Pete Reever coming in.

Slipping into the shadows, Dennis stood and watched, to make sure. Pete Reever in the Eagle! The ironworker stepped up to the bar, ordered a pop, turned, and surveyed the room as if he could get anyone in it. This proves, Dennis thought, that a lot of working-class macho is a mask. A mask; or it proves that there's no such thing as straight. But if there's no straight then there's no gay. Anyway, the main thing it proves is that if Dennis doesn't get Mike the hell out of there before he sees Pete Reever, everybody dies.

Slipping around the back way into the other room to yank Mike out onto the street, Dennis panicked for a moment when he couldn't find him—no, *there,* in the corner, talking, with a look of grave ire on his face, to a gym-inflated boy wearing ropes on his torso instead of a shirt.

"Let's split," Dennis told Mike, his mind on the back exit.

"Do you mind?" cried the rope boy. "The dude and I are having a conversation."

Dennis took Mike's arm, and the rope boy shoved Dennis.

"You touch him again, you faggot," said Mike, "and I'll kick your cocksucking head in."

Dennis called him every week, dreading the impatient voice he'd get, the burly manner. Maybe I should have let him see Pete Reever in his element, he thought, shaken him up good. One week Dennis didn't call, and a few days later Mike rang up, said, "Where the hell were you last week, you fucking jackoff?" and hung up.

Then Dennis turned twenty, and took everyone out to dinner, and announced that he had found a place, and they all drank to it, and Mike asked how much a month, and Dennis said, "I'm buying it," and Mike grew as silent as Vesuvius resenting the noise coming over from Pompeii. And let us not forget Aunt Molleen's suspicion of Jews, and Erica's suspicion of the Irish, and Mike's suspicion of gays, and Dennis thinking he doesn't owe anyone an apology for living, and we have a dinner somewhat less than delightful. Then Erica tries to get a bit of spin going by asking Dennis about the music business, and Aunt Molleen chimes in and the three of them are pushing it along nicely when Erica proposes they toast Dennis' precocious success.

As she raised her wine, Dennis caught in her eyes the sincerity of her hopes, hopes for all of them, toward sound health and good works and dear loves. Or was it naught but wine reflected there, shimmering, promising? No, Aunt Molleen saw something too. "There's a blessing on you for saying it," she told Erica, and, teetotal, raised her water glass. But Mike only sat there, his arms on the table edge and his mouth an expressionist painter's idea of irony.

"I don't need your approval," said Dennis.

"That's good," said Mike, "because you ain't getting it."

Silence. The glasses dropped back upon the table.

"And how's everything here?" said their waiter, wandering up.

Mike and Dennis glared at each other. Aunt Molleen did a little business with her napkin. "It's fine, thank you," said Erica. As the waiter withdrew, she went on, "You boys can settle this any way you want. I just want you to know that it hurts my heart to see two brothers fighting when they're old enough to be men. It hurts my heart."

Silence.

"I'm a stranger here myself," Erica noted, turning to Dennis. "But I think it's fairly obvious that you do need Michael's approval." Now she got Mike. "And you need his."

"Like fuck I do."

"Parnell Michael Keogh," said Aunt Molleen.

"I haven't done anything wrong, Iron Mike," said Dennis.

Why does he call him that? Erica wondered.

Mike shook his head.

"Please," said Erica.

"Yeah," Dennis added.

"A fine pass we've come to," said Aunt Molleen, "to hear such talk in a family."

Mike, one of those who feels it inopportune to back down once he's staked out his position, only grows harder. Iron Mike, the most excellent boy in the neighborhood. "A fine pass," says Mike, "to have a brother selling out his people for the caviar faggots who own this country."

"Writing songs? You call that selling out? Hit songs?"

"The disco kid!"

"You work your ass off building palaces for the lawyers and the bankers! And I'm the sellout?"

"I get pay for work, not for partying. Huh?"

"Nevertheless."

"Is that how your new friends talk? 'Nevertheless'?"

"Stop it, the two of you!" Aunt Molleen whispered. "Stop and an end to this!" A start of fear sharpened her face, as if she was in sudden pain, but she looked down and became calm. "And me so proud of you, flesh of my own sister's flesh, the only things she left on earth. And the police asking me why she died." A fit of coughing overtook her, but she shook it off. "Why she died. Who knows why?"

The Witch knows. Johnny knows. Dennis knows. All others who knew are dead.

"And your brother Johnny off on his own, burying your father without a word to us till after, freeze him in the earth, and no one to drink him his last voyage. And some not speaking to others. All this anger." She coughed briefly. "Who needs the Brits for a curse when we've our own to put it on us?"

It was Erica, alone of the other three, who realized that Aunt Molleen was ailing—had surely been for months now, and said nothing of it to any of them. Erica searched for Mike's hand under the table. He took it, tightly, and did not look at her or anyone.

"It's enough now," Aunt Molleen concluded.

"It's enough," said Mike.

"I'll say," Dennis put in.

"Let's all go home," said Erica.

"And how are we doing tonight?" the waiter uttered, gliding up with the check.

Mike and Dennis said no more on any of the matters at hand, and they tacitly agreed not to retain their weekly phone calls, perhaps to let some time heal their differences. And they doubtless would have settled these if only José the hustler had not opened the door, nude, at full mast, to mistake Mike for the other hustler they'd ordered on the night Aunt Molleen had her heart attack.

The first problem was that they had unplugged the phone, bringing Mike to Dennis' apartment to break the news and take him to the hospital. The second was that José is basically a human cock—take it away and there's not much left. So the sight of him grinning at the door and crying out, "Dennis, look what they sent —an Italian shitkicker!" does not enchant your homophobic brother. The third problem was that Dennis was nude and grinning, too, till he saw who was standing in the doorway looking like Moses about to shatter the tablets.

As Aunt Molleen would have said, "Esh." Like Nora, however, she never uttered a last word.

There was no wake, just a burial, way out on Long Island. Erica was not there. Mike was not speaking to Dennis. After the others left, the two of them stood side by side facing the grave, their loyalties fiercely enmeshed and clashing. Finally Mike turned away. Dennis followed.

"I'd like to send the limo away and ride back with you," he told Mike.

"In a pickup, fancy boy? You'd muss your suit."

"Please don't do this."

"I don't want you in my truck."

Mike started on; Dennis stayed with him. "How about declaring peace for a day in Aunt Molleen's memory? We can break the war out again tomorrow."

Mike said nothing. As they approached the parking lot, he

strode toward an emerald-green pickup truck with a shamrock on the door. Dennis darted to the side, told his driver to take off, and hopped into the truck just as Mike started pulling out. They rode in silence for twenty minutes, both looking straight ahead. Then Mike said, "Let's stop for some chow."

They studied the dinner menus as if they'd never seen such before, uncertain of what to do when the waitress reclaimed them and they'd have to confront each other.

Suddenly Mike began to talk. He had left the ironworkers' union to get into steel and iron, and went on in smooth detail about the cost of labor, materials, delays, the corruption and fixing. He went on till they left the table. Back in the truck, they drove in silence again, Mike defeating all Dennis' gambits with grunts, and said perfunctory goodbyes when Mike paused in front of Dennis' building.

Thirty minutes later, Dennis charged out of his apartment, ran the eight blocks to Mike's, and stood staring at the entrance. As someone came out, Dennis pushed in, climbed the stairs, and banged on Mike's door.

"Let me in!"

Mike in the doorway.

"I won't have this stupid quarrel anymore," said Dennis, keeping his eyes clean of anxiety. "It's about nothing."

Mike doesn't move.

"Come on, Iron Mike."

Mike lets Dennis in.

"Now you can tell me just what it is you're afraid of."

Mike stares at Dennis.

"Because you're afraid of something, right? Otherwise, why are you freezing me out?"

They stand eye to eye like gunslingers.

"It's not the gay thing," Dennis went on. "And it's not because I'm moving with a fancy crowd. What is it?"

Mike stood there.

"Tell me." Dennis heard his voice gulp, and steeled himself. "Okay, I'll guess. I'm doing better than you. I'm making a lot of money and I'll make a lot more. Who knows? Millions. You can't stand that, can you? You always have to be older and stronger and more important than everyone else in the room, don't you? Big man, the big man, Iron Mike. Having an older brother who landed on skid row or wherever he is now suits you fine. But a younger brother who ends up a hot shot makes you insecure. Threatens the big man. He calls me the disco kid, puts me in my place. But, let me tell you, I'm doing what I want to do and I'm taking orders from no one and it's going to turn out real profitable, despite a certain disadvantage in my birth. Whether you like it or not."

You could have set paper afire by holding it before Mike's eyes, but he said nothing.

"A disadvantage in my birth," Dennis repeated, knowing that somehow this tormented Mike. "A wacked-out family of losers and drifters who don't know how to be there when it counts."

"Are you going to blame ma?" Mike said at last. "Because she was harsh with us sometimes? You gays always get around to blaming your mothers sooner or later, don't you?"

"No one's to blame. It's probably genetic. And blame? Who's to *blame* that you're straight?"

" 'Nevertheless.' "

"And saying she was harsh is a euphemism."

Mike folded his arms across his chest. "I fucking dare you to explain that, buddy boy."

"Nora loved you. But not Johnny or me. She wasn't harsh. She was cold, selfish, and crazy."

Mike moved toward Dennis, checked himself, backed off, pointed at him. "Get out of my house, you faggot, or I'll fucking deck you and throw you out."

"I'm not moving."

"I'm warning you."

"We're not going to settle this till you work your rage off, so go ahead and deck me."

"You have five seconds."

Dennis folded his arms across his chest.

Mike started counting; at three, the phone rang. Mike answered,

162

smiled, and went into that good-time soft-mouth men use with women who amuse them. After letting Dennis stand around like a decoration for some time, he told him, over his shoulder, "This'll take a while, so blow."

And Dennis did.

From the day he set out his first posters, Johnny's version of Steel Fist, called The Great Event, made him happy and caused him trouble—happier than the presentation of such brutality should make a man, and more trouble than such a simple enterprise should be. Lucrative it surely was, minimal expenditure yielding a heavy gate. But it seems that the professional, regular, publicly apparent organization of man-to-man battle falls into syndicate territory, and the syndicate is never glad to take in an alien, no matter what dues he pays. The occasional Hibernian Steel Fist the syndicate would blink as it might a John L. Sullivan club. But an advertised series of bare-knuckles contests touring a circuit from Long Island to New Jersey was a challenge to entrenched structures, and a drain on the wrestling and boxing economy.

Johnny had a visit from a youngish, engaging big man in a dark suit, suggesting he desist.

Johnny said nothing to him, and showed nothing. Listened. Didn't even nod perfunctorily.

The man in the suit did not intend to fight it out at the time, and made an unnuanced exit. No warning envoi or foreboding pat on the cheek. He left.

Now there will be a meeting, and grumbling from the older dark suits, and, to put it mildly, scuffles.

So Johnny sends word: we will talk. At the park at the end of Fifty-third Street, a weekday, noon. They come; so. They talk. They want sixty percent.

Twenty. Johnny.

Sixty. Who he thinks he is?

Twenty. I have the magic.

So fifty. You could be dead.

Twenty-five, and that's already too much.

We're crazy even to talk about it. Fifty.

No.

Fifty or you could meet the fish.

Thirty. That's the top.

Forty.

Johnny thinks. He can always cheat them down to thirty. They probably expect it. He doesn't like hooking up with a mob. Gives him the whispers. But the idea's too hot to drop.

Forty, Johnny agrees.

Their stupid smiles. How did they get so powerful? Guinzos. A lot of fat-assed guinzos. Guns and manpower is all they have, families. Generations. Generations of guinzos loyal to each other and to hell with the world, pushing their bellies against you. Guinzos like Mike.

The Firing Gun told Dennis he had reached a *People* 19 level, with an IM 72 and a hot +.

That is: as subject for the cover of *People* magazine, if an established star is level 1 ("extremely marketistic") and a relatively minor assassin is level 6 ("mischievously enticing"), and last year's astronaut is level 30 ("nostalgically revivable"), and your high-school French teacher is level 428 ("non-potential"), Dennis was a contender. His IM (Identification rating, classification in Music) was, out of 1 to 100, well beyond distinguished obscurity if short of true fame. The hot scale registered only plus or minus: potential or exhausted, pass or fail. Dennis was passing.

He was so urbane that when an actor up for an Emmy for a mini-series asked Dennis, apparently joking, what he should say to make himself memorable if he won, Dennis replied that a very short and objectionable speech not antagonizing any of the major racial, religious, or ideological minorities would make him the talk of the industry.

"Like what?" the actor said.

"Like who's favored for the award?"

The actor pranced like a rooster. "If not me? Who?"

"If not you. Who else?"

The actor shrugged. "Ed Asner."

"He'll probably win. But if you do, admire the hardware, beam sardonically at America and say, 'I'd like to thank Ed Asner for losing.' "

"Hey, that's right!"

"No. That's crude and stupid. All the just people in show biz will despise you—both of them. The others will love your guts and talk you up to heaven. Meanwhile, there'll be a national storm. You humbly apologize. And that's fame." The Firing Gun couldn't have called it more aptly.

But The Firing Gun was fame's scientist and Dennis, now, its critic. He coined the term "schlockerize": to assimilate one's talent into a schedule of success. The honchos picked up on it, and used it—to mean "to make love to the demographics and produce a hit." Dennis urbanely schlockerized, because then everybody liked him.

Bill was more urbane than Dennis, though of course he had seen a great deal more of the world. He had been several things to many people, any role; that was his living. Amazing endurance. Every so often Ardie would snarl at him and important visitors would delicately regret the imminent departure of Bill Fears. Yet he stayed on, year after year, as Dennis wrote and Carla sang and their fame interfaced so trimly that, long after Ardie's group had given up pretending the two musicians were even speaking, they were taken by the public for husband and wife.

A reliable whore can be indispensable in a palace. Ardie had learned that those hungry, beautiful boys with astonishing behinds eventually start cheating, over-coking, and stealing, while an Ivy Leaguer like Bill could be depended on and taken anywhere. Besides, he was useful in keeping Dennis safe. The role of the companion is an important one in many a tale, though of course a discreet storyteller will draw a curtain over their lingering glances and clammy sighs. It is told that the poet Prince of Tara took along a confidant when the Scornful Witch of Fooley imprisoned the Prince in a high tower on the shores of the western sea after her chess game with the King his father. Strange: the King thought he had won. Nine years, we know, the Prince spent in his tower, and when at last he rejoined his people, he was wise: for in his isolation, and through speculative dialogue with his companion, the Prince had learned to contemplate the world.

"Why aren't you a writer?" Dennis asked Bill as they sat on Dennis' terrace. "With all your smarts?"

"Because I don't care," Bill told him.

"You sure care a lot of ideas on me when we talk."

"Mere repartee."

"Then what are you going to do, ever? Just this?"

"Physician, heal thyself."

Dennis rose and examined the street below. "So many people," he said. "Think of all the stories. Yet they say there are only three tales—that everything is a variation or a combination of one or another. The revenge. The romance. The quest." He turned to Bill. "You don't approve of my work, do you?"

"Not yet."

Dennis nodded. "So when?"

"When you stop taking it easy and use what you have. When you make something."

"I *make* . . ." Dennis began, floundering, with a bite of anger. "I make hits."

"You should make something so unique that if you hadn't lived, there'd be a gap in the histories of your field. That's worth a try, isn't it?"

Dennis comically moaned, grasping the railing as he beckoned to Bill. "Come look," said Dennis.

The street. It was five something on a weekday afternoon, early fall, something cooking inside each coat as it cantered out of the office and homeward, or to dinner or some show. Come look at the sheer numbers, the weight of people. Bill stood beside Dennis. "In all that pack down there," Dennis said, "there's only three stories. Three, plus variations and combinations. So how much unique can there be in one world? How many gaps to close?"

"Jargon," said Bill. "Semantic Chinese-box evasionism. You are what you do."

"So where does that leave my Uncle Flaherty, I wonder? All he ever does is what the rest of his union did. They built buildings.

They took the iron and bulled it up in some kind of order and tied it together, and now you and I and the rest of the world have somewhere to go when it's cold. He isn't unique, right? He doesn't seal a gap. But without the Uncle Flahertys of this world you'd freeze your tail off. Or no—why get metaphorical about it? Without Uncle Flaherty, there'd be no New York. He made it, and his kind. And the iron. I know it. I don't mention it much, and to tell the truth Uncle Flaherty never had much use for me. But I know it. Because I come from a building family. Sure, we're just the proles of it, the team players. And now one of us is conked out because he's a bad mean son of a bitch. And I fell into the sweet life, didn't I? But this other one—he'll be a builder, head of the team. He may not be unique but he'll close a gap. This block. Another block. He'll build high and heavy so all these crazy New Yorkers can fit in this little place we got here. Right now money's tight and they're holding back. But watch what happens in a few years. By 1980 they'll be shooting this town to the moon. That's what we do, Bill. And I know he'll be on top of it, because he's not the kind who takes orders from other men. Or anything else from them. See, Mike kind of likes to be the only male in the joint, you know what I mean? He gets kind of uncomfortable around other men's power. Other men's money. Other men's sensuality. I figured that out myself. Aren't I smart?"

They were staring down at the street.

"The revenge," Bill echoed. "The romance. The quest. That makes you what, the quest?"

Dennis shrugged. "Sure, why not?"

"Then why aren't you seeking something?"

"Like what?"

"Like a reconciliation with your brother. Like hot art. Like a way around the Firing Gun's celeb charts. Like liberty."

Bill gave him a long look. Dennis shook his head; but Bill looked more, and hard.

"Don't do that," said Dennis.

"They'll dry you out," said Bill. "Then you won't care, either."

I care plenty, man.

"Or why aren't you in love right now?" Bill went on. "Why

don't you have friends? You had them when you were a kid, didn't you?"

Dennis walked into the kitchen and pulled the refrigerator open. "Cheese," he said. "Cold cuts. Several kinds of milk. Hershey bars. Capers." He pulled the bottle of capers out. He called to Bill, "I have the most incredible maid. I say, 'Get something tasty at D'Agostino, Elsie.' And she buys capers."

Bill was silent, coming through the apartment.

"Now what I really seek in the world is toast. Four slices, with sweet butter, cut diagonally." In the cupboard. "See, we've got white, rye, raisin-date, whole wheat . . . oh that stupid Elsie, she forgot to buy toast!"

Bill put a hand on Dennis' shoulder.

"I can't force myself on him if he won't see me," said Dennis, without moving. His eyes were closed. "You don't know what he's like. And since when are brothers the great salvation, huh? You grow up and shed them, like your fifteen-year-old's awkwardness and your neighborhood accent." Dennis turned to face Bill. "The family is defunct, so leave it alone. If I can't be rich, famous, and loved, I'll be rich. I never wanted to be famous, anyway. You can be my brother, now. Maybe that's what all gays should do when they come out—adopt a brother and screw the Mary and Joseph out of him."

"You could write him a letter."

"I wrote, man. Several times. I *wrote!* He doesn't answer."

"Maybe he—"

"Bill. Leave it alone. Please? Okay? Everyone wants me to do something now. Carla's been at me to take her dancing because she hasn't been in a column in the last three minutes. Ardie says my songs are edging into black comedy."

"Whistle for me."

"What?"

"You know. Those signals you—"

"That's the second time today someone asked me to whistle."

"Who else?"

"A baglady near the skating rink. I gave her the old All Clear

168

and she cackled. Then she asked me if I had any hot secrets to share. She said, 'Call up someone you love and tell him a wicked secret.' Isn't New York wonderful?"

"Why not write a song about it?"

"Come on. Can you see Carla singing about a baglady? I'm the maestro of a *mellow* cabaret, remember?"

"Does Carla have to sing everything you write?"

You run with the mob, you do your job efficiently. That's what they need; grandstanders, kite flyers, worry them. They want solid, dependable, routine. No wind, no suction, no running with it. Yet Johnny cannot help but put on a brilliant show. He's Kid Danger and this is his Great Event, his Saturday Special. He's got to jive it through. Return bouts. Favorites, champions with nicknames. The Slicer. Grunting Grover. The Great Carnivore. And everybody defers to Johnny; or everybody better. He walks into the arena during setup and it's like the general inspecting the battleship and the take is heavy—or, as they say in boxing, the gate is swinging wide. So the boys are a little anxious. That's their natural condition; anyway, it's worth their while. Men want to slam each other into pulp, who should stop them?

Because there's money in it. Because men like to fight. Because life is intemperate.

Erica was pregnant, Mike was overjoyed, and the two of them were married at City Hall. They moved into Erica's apartment, by far the better of the two, sunnier and roomier; and made plans to lay their traces in the vaster terrain beyond Manhattan's moat. While sorting through a box of papers, Erica happened upon a small batch of letters clumped in a rubber band, all from Dennis to Mike. She read them. They were badly typed and somewhat stiff in expression, mainly about the music business and L.A. and swimming pool parties and other irrelevant things. Mike blundered in, bearing that rotten old armchair he had refused to part with; he wiped his forehead with the bottom of his sweater.

"What are you reading?"

"They appear to be a least-favored nation's diplomatic correspondence suing for recognition."

"Huh? Half the time I . . . Oh, yeah . . . yeah, he . . . he used to write so we should stay in touch, you know? How about the chair up here, like, aimed at the TV, so—"

"You didn't answer them, did you?"

"Nope. Like this, see? Easy on the eye, soft on the butt."

"How could you not answer his letters? Michael, let go! Don't you care how he must feel?"

"What answer? I can't write letters."

"You could call him."

"So why should I?"

"How long has it been since you two have spoken?"

"Who's counting?"

Erica read from the letter she had been holding when Mike came in: " 'I hope you're making progress in your career and if you ever need a loan of some kind, for example if you wanted working capital or whatever like that, you can always ask me because I have some money I don't need. Be sure to say hello to Erica for me. Very truly yours, Dennis.' "

"Look. I don't want his cocaine faggot money, okay?"

" 'Very truly yours.' Your own brother is afraid to sign 'Love.' How long has it been, Michael? That dinner at Lüchow's, when the two of you had a fight? What was that, four years ago?"

Mike shook his head. "Aunt Molleen's funeral. He was there."

"You haven't spoken to him since *then?*"

Mike pulled the armchair into its chosen corner. He sat, sighting the television screen. He got up and adjusted it, sighted again, and sat there, tired and sweaty.

"Sweetheart," he began. He stopped, looked away. "Jesus Mary. I been trying to call him."

"Michael."

"Started when Uncle Flaherty died. I thought, no matter what's between us, he should know about it, and see him off. He was a good old guy, anyway, though he and little brother never had much to do with each other, I guess." Mike cleared his throat. "So I called. And I got this tape thing with someone else's voice, like a male secretary. 'All calls are screened,' or something. First time, I thought it was a wrong number. But I kept getting it, so I thought, fuck that. I'm not talking to no tape thing. He wants to speak to me, he can come to the phone like a man."

"A lot of people do that now. To screen out crank calls."

"Yeah. Like from their brothers? No, honey, listen. I kept calling and getting the tape. So, like, I waited a while, and then I called and this phone company voice comes on that the number is disconnected and there's no further information on it. So okay. And meanwhile he's writing these letters. So all right. If he doesn't want to call, let him write down what his secret new tape number is, okay?"

"And?"

Mike stretched. He had worked a long day and hefted furniture all evening. "And? And what? And nothing." His brow darkened, drew taut. He did not tell Erica that he had dropped in on Dennis' apartment and found that he had moved. Nor did he speak of the night not so long before, when, reading in the *Post* that Carla Feller would be doing Studio, Mike turned up, flashed a bill, and pushed in to find Dennis. From ten o'clock, Mike stood around in a crowd of people who looked as if their clothes were made of the flesh of babies, as if they had never heard, and would not have believed, that there was a population of Americans who labor instead of dancing and taking drugs for a living. Weary and disgusted, he had stumbled home at one A.M., not realizing that A-List folk make late, thus grand, entrances. Two hours after Mike departed the scene, Ardie's gang swept in, Dennis walking in bitty steps like a prisoner chained at the ankles.

"And nothing. That's it."

It's not the guinzos who are the problem, Johnny thought, counting the take, subtracting the percentage, turning the local champions into regional champions, one on another, blood after blood, with no end possible and the whole scheme promising millions after due expansion. It's not the guinzos. Because the Great Event was so profitable that they finally began to relax. It didn't even cut into their boxing-and-wrestling crap; too different—vicious where boxing was competitive, and spontaneous where wrestling was theatrical. They took their fucking time about coming together on it, okay, three years, four. Something. But they got there.

So it's not the guinzos. It's the fighters. They don't grasp the purity of the sportsman's amateur standing, free of taint. Trouble is, they're a success. Got fan clubs, even, some of them. So naturally they come bucking for a piece of the action. Knowledge of just who Johnny's allies are keeps them from bucking too hard. Still, it's a raid on one's energy.

"I'm not in this for my health," The Great Carnivore growls one night after a particularly eventful Great Event during which four contestants were sent to the hospital and one was temporarily blinded.

"You don't like the terms," says Johnny, taking a ready stance, "get the fuck out of it." Five takes two he backs off.

"I don't like your fucking face," The Great Carnivore points out, not backing off, and clearly taking the measure of Johnny's physique as if deciding which parts to break first. The other men in the dressing room move back to give them plenty of room.

Johnny smiles. He beckons. He whispers. "I dare you."

The Great Carnivore would be a fool to try it. He's half dressed, for one thing, so all Johnny has to do is catch him up in his trousers and he'll be helpless. For another, there are Johnny's clodhoppers, which, The Great Carnivore figures, will go on a tour of his balls. Not to mention the mob meatheads who will be requested thereafter to uphold a little discipline upon The Great Carnivore's person.

"All right, forget it," The Great Carnivore grunts, relaxing.

"I ain't forgetting nothing," Johnny tells him, never prone to leave a battle unfought. "Fucking shithead jackoff coward. You're out. As of. Pack up and blow."

A great stillness in the room. All eyes on Johnny, who looks as he did when he told Dennis of his army of mice, and Dennis struggled to get away, and Johnny held him fast and said he would summon them to take Dennis to their secret torture chamber. The Great Carnivore is now officially backed off for good, but a mean dark light in his eyes warns Johnny there'll be somewhat more to follow.

Dennis got tipsy and decided the hell with it and looked Mike up in the phone book. He wasn't there. Nor was Uncle Flaherty, which was odd—to Dennis, who had no idea that he was dead. And of course Dennis wasn't in the book, either. There were a goodly number of Keoghs, but none of the right ones. We're written out of the world, Dennis thought: not even among the plebes in their golden book that tells all citizens but the vagrants that somebody knows their name. A great list of kind with challenging omissions. Erica, for instance. Could she have married Mike and moved with him to the suburbs? Dennis tried information for all communicative regions; no Mike. He tried the ironworkers' union—had a Parnell Michael Keogh left a forwarding address?

"We get these calls for a lot of the men," said the guy who answered. "But not usually from another man, you know?"

"This is his brother," said Dennis.

"Yeah, that happens," the union guy told him, quite sincerely. "Death in the family?"

"Not as far as I know."

All they had was Mike's old address and phone number, anyway. "Sometimes," the man told Dennis, "if you like try the how-you-might-say cast-off girlfriends. You'd be surprised how they can stay in touch."

That night Dennis left for L.A.

Johnny was living with a woman named Wendy who called him Candy Cane and never got enough. When he brooded, she'd rub his back and thighs and spread his legs and tickle him until he was on her again. She had a thing about chairs. Any time Johnny was in a good mood, he'd ask her if she wanted anything, and she'd snap back, "Ball me in a chair."

She has another thing about families, such as asking questions

Johnny could do without. At times he'll tell her a tale or two, in which he is a sort of blundering decent fellow abused by grungy relations. Do we believe the tales we tell? Johnny believes his. When Wendy asks where they all are now, he earnestly replies, "Who gives a fuck? What do I need them for now? What did I ever?"

Except when he dreams, and they are all there, chasing past him, or running from him. He cannot move or speak. The sad truth of it is that we do need them for something, and a great sage of the modern day, who interpreted many a saga as its subjects sat in his office, fuming, warns us that those who are denied this something may not be able to love or work satisfactorily. We need them. Some mornings, Johnny awakens with the memory of his ma dancing with Dennis so bright in his head he almost comes out of the bedroom to see if they are there, and it will be a moment or two before he can shake it off.

Mike had the brilliant idea of writing to Dennis through an address he found on one of Carla Feller's albums. Saying nothing to Erica, he sat down early one morning before he left for work and painfully scratched out a rough draft in pencil. He told of his career and his marriage. He said he hoped Dennis was fine. He did not want to write more than this; he wanted Dennis to reply, and they could then meet and talk, for Mike felt he was a better talker than letter writer. But he knew there was something else he must say. As the minutes crept past, he tried it every which way, and it never sounded right. Sometimes it came out as if Mike was alibiing. Other times it came out as if Mike was condemning Dennis while he exonerated him. Big words will do that to you.

So finally Mike just wrote it straight, which was, "I am sorry that I got sore at you because you are gay. Instead, I should have been there for you, but I wasn't. Please accept my apology because you will always be who you are, which is my brother. And that is what counts. And now that we are the only ones left in our family, it is really bad that we don't see each other. So let's get together and maybe we can talk it out and shake hands and be friends again, which is what we should be."

He didn't know how to close it. "Your brother, Mike" sounded distant. "Love, Mike" was absurd. It occurred to him to put down, "Your straight brother, Iron Mike"—and he couldn't think of why that seemed exactly right, but he knew it was.

So he wrote that and folded it up, and he gave it to the girl in the office to type for him, though he knew it would get around about what he had said. Hell, he might as well get used to people knowing he has this gay brother. And off the letter went.

Four weeks later, he received a form postcard thanking him for submitting material and regretting that they already had more than they could handle.

It was now very nearly seven years since Mike and Dennis had seen each other.

Now, all the ancient sagas favor a certain moment when an important warrior faces an overwhelming ambush, and, while the reader knows that the hero must fall before the unfortunate odds, he himself fights as if invincible—which, all things considered, he virtually has been up to that point. Often, he will remark casually on the irony of life as he falls, whereupon the narrator or bard or scribe will move on as discreetly and quickly as possible, saying only that now the hero is out of the saga.

It is usual for this confrontation of one against a crowd to be the work of vengeance, to repay the warrior for a murder, or a victory in a duel, or even for an uncharitable comment designed to make a man look foolish. So it was here, when Johnny cut through the alley behind the arena house to get to his car, as he habitually did at the end of a Great Event. Routine of time and place is a vainglory for those with enemies, but Johnny had never been one to schedule sensible defenses; like a true hero, he took each thing as it came, fatalistically. Anyway, as he saw it, he had the world for an enemy. Why make detours when every turning of the road may hide hostile troops? Six steps from the door, he saw two huge thugs slide up out of the shadows, and from perhaps six feet behind him The Great Carnivore said, "I don't forget nothing, either, pal!"

He's too close, Johnny thought, pulling out his gun. The Great Carnivore is too fast as well, and grabs for the metal as his two

henchmen run up. If they reach Johnny thus occupied, it's all over
—whatever happens, must happen at exactly this moment, so
Johnny kicks at The Great Carnivore's shin, and he goes down with
a scream. But the other two get to Johnny before he can whirl with
the gun. One takes hold of the piece. The other pulls Johnny's head
back from behind, and he's kicking out at the front guy, thinking
any second his neck is going to snap, and the gun goes off once,
again, but no one's hit, and suddenly Johnny flops over as if he
had fallen off a chair and the two of them are going at him, one
bare-handed and one with the piece. Johnny can hear their panting
as he flips over and ooches around just right and with a cry he's
on his feet again—no, that always worked before, but these guys
are too good, ten years and fifty pounds advantage on him, each.
He should be on his feet, but he's on his back, totally vulnerable.
He tries to turn over and protect his head, but they lovingly pull
him over again on his back and stretch him out and they're laughing because The Great Carnivore is back among the living and he
wants his inning. Sometimes these grudge matches get out of
control, and The Great Carnivore, breathing fire, wades into
Johnny like there's no next Wednesday and the other two pick up
the rhythm The Great Carnivore hears and they're all in it, stomp-
ing the boy to death.

That's all he is, a boy: though he has held a man's estate of
passing among ruthless males on full terms for over a decade. Not
a sound came out of Johnny at the end, not even a cry for his ma.
But he thought of her. He saw her dancing somewhere, alone, in
a room, turning to the music, and, seeing something of great
interest, she drew toward it, and extended her arms, not smiling,
and Johnny figured he was the one she saw. That was how she
always looked to him: curious, expectant, grim. To feel of him and
know him. That was how she looked. And then he lost conscious-
ness, and an hour later he was dead.

So there was no ironic comment from him. But the Witch
phrased it well in his place, saying, "That will have been Kid
Danger's very own Saturday Special."

And now he is out of the saga.

*   *   *

176

The advantage in schlockerizing was that once everybody got used to you, almost anything you did had to succeed, because no one in America really listened and therefore liked anything associated with an amiable name. And thus passed a few more years of Tara, as Dennis shuffled between New York and L.A., the two stages of the electro-technical American media theatre, and made no friends, and believed in nothing, and wrote songs, quite spontaneously, that protected his feelings from scrutiny. "A Waltz for My Mother," the song he had promised Nora over a decade before, was Carla Feller's biggest hit, and every time Dennis heard it he mimed barfing. Enough is enough, so he wrote "Deep-Pocket Party," autobiographically:

> . . . And they grease their wheels on lingo,
> The native and the pipsqueak gringo,
> As a model proposes his abs;
> Or they do their deals in foyers,
> The connectors and the destroyers,
> And the cowboys are coming in cabs!

"I hate it," said Carla, in Ardie's Hollywood home, folding a page of *Rolling Stone* into a funny hat.

Dennis liked L.A. Except for Carla and The Firing Gun, everyone in L.A. was nice to him.

"Den," said Carla, leaping into the tender vocative as she would, "we need happy disco genre. What is this with destroyers?"

L.A. doesn't like satire.

"This isn't New York," Carla pursued, "where everyone enjoys being grumpy."

L.A. was possibly good for you.

"Destroyers, I mean!"

As a lobotomy is good for a recurring nightmare; but everyone is nice to you.

"Schlockerize it, Dennis," Ardie advised. "It's rough."

"Look at me," said Carla, modeling her hat.

"Get pervasive," The Firing Gun told Dennis. "Hectic. Discable."

On the contrary, Dennis got restless, needful, rebellious. After nearly nine years of being pretentious but popular, why not try being direct if unpleasant? He gave "Deep-Pocket Party" to the drugabilly semi-heavy-metal group Mission Insufferable and had almost as big a hit as with "A Waltz for My Mother." The Firing Gun was furious, but Ardie thought it an amusing escapade, till Dennis wrote another not entirely polite salute to American arts life, "The Hot Man Cometh," and quietly gave it to Gary Entry. Another hit. Odd, Dennis thought: writing sincerely is as easy as writing flattery.

On the other hand, everyone was mad at him now, on and off. No one in media is ever completely mad at anyone who makes a lot of money. But, anyway, what did Dennis have to lose and who cares who gets mad at you? What did he need them for? Huh, he would say, his latest thing. *Huh.*

"You're neglecting Carla, boy," The Firing Gun warned him. She notices these things. "Get *with* it."

"Huh," said Dennis.

"It's getting awfully complicated," said Ardie, "about image, boy wonder. We don't want a crooked image, now, do we?"

"I skew image," said Dennis in fluent media. "Huh."

"Den," Carla suggested, "be a boyfriend and stop like—"

"Huh," said Dennis. "Huh, Carla."

"He's raving."

Sometimes he was. Then someone had the idea to cap a comedy film set in Manhattan with a big musical number shot on location amid the traffic and the office buildings and lunchtime gawkers. A kind of rock video in apotheosis. The hook was that many several celebs would take part at scale. The PR would be, as The Firing Gun put it, "Maybe frightening." She thought it would be cute if Dennis turned up to sing a line or two with Carla.

Dennis said no, I can't sing or dance.

"You'll schlockerize it," said Ardie, his hands wide. The trouble they give one to make them happy.

Dennis, idling at the piano, said he'd look like an idiot.

Carla enthusiastically agreed.

The Firing Gun said that's not the point.

"Gwen Verdon," said Ardie. "Robert Preston. Debra Winger. Julie Andrews. Dudley Moore. Angela Lansbury. Ginger Rogers. John Rubinstein—"

"They're performers. I'm not."

"*Thumbscrew* him!" cried The Firing Gun.

"Imagine having to force someone to be in a movie," said Carla, truly awed.

"Listen," said Dennis, improvising a folkish strain:

> *As I came down to the market town,*
> *As I came into the city,*
> *I met a man who kills for a fee;*
> *He showed me a skull*
> *And said, That's me*
> *If I dare enter the city.*

"What do you think?"

"Shut up, I think," said Ardie.

"See what I mean?" Carla put in. "These new songs of his. He shows him a skull? Who would sing that?"

"Come on," said Dennis. "They love it when I do skulls. I'm going to make my career on the death of love and glamor."

"How rude," said Ardie.

"Love and glamor never died," offered Carla. "They're in Wyoming doing retakes."

"Who wrote that for her?" asked Dennis.

"Darling, I spit on you."

"Movie," said Ardie.

"Huh."

"Movie, boy wonder."

"Not boy wonder. The disco kid."

Ardie grinned. "I like it."

One day Bill Fears told Dennis that he was leaving. Dennis, who had this one friend and no other, kept asking why and could not be told. A connector has many jobs, all secret.

"Listen," said Bill, "don't let them finesse you. Trap you."

"It's not money, is it?" asked Dennis, panicked into rudeness.

"This is not what gay is," Bill told him. "This is just another outfit in the Corporation. I think you know that now. I can tell by your songs. I can tell by the corners of Ardie's mouth. I can tell by the pills Carla's taking. I can tell by the color The Firing Gun's been turning lately."

"Terrific. Everyone I like walks out on me and everyone I loathe hangs on and shoves me around. Ardie and Firing want me to be in this movie thing because—"

"You will be in it."

"*Huh.* You, too?"

"I found your brother."

Dennis froze, relaxed, and shook his head, tried to smile, walked away. "Oh yeah, is that so?"

"Dennis."

"You're really something, can I say so? You're really a choice item."

Bill started for him, but Dennis gave him the straight arm.

"No! No, just a . . . just . . . walk out, right, and drop a bombshell on me on your way! Hey, what is that, my . . . my *tip?* Or don't I tip you, hustler?"

"You be good or else," said Bill. "Isn't that what your brother would say?"

"Sure." Dennis started to cry. "What do you mean you found him?"

Bill held him. "Everything's written down somewhere if you know where to look."

"Where is he, anyway?"

Bill rubbed Dennis' neck. "Long Island."

"I already tried him there. No."

"He's got everything listed under his company, not his name."

Dennis stood back, holding Bill's arms. "His company?"

"He went into business with a building contractor. Small firm. Very lucrative. The contractor had the capital and knows cost.

That's the key to the business, did your brother ever tell you that? Stop grimacing and listen. You have to know in advance how much each sector of a job will cost, so you can collect profit to the penny. The man had the capital and the cost down, but he needed someone to handle the work on the sites. Your brother held out for a full partnership, and they reformed the company. Even renamed it—"

"*Jesus*, man, who *are* you?"

Bill smiled. "I'm one of your connectors." He sometimes made these outlandish statements.

"The connectors . . ." said Dennis. "And the destroyers . . ."

"You have nothing to cry about. It's almost over. Trust me."

"I'm crying because I never wanted to grow up. You know? Some people have such a terrible childhood they can't wait to get old. But I should have stayed ten for forty years. That's what I was good for—whistling with Mark Revien and sneaking into theatres. New York stuff. So why am I in L.A.?"

Bill wiped Dennis' cheeks with his fingers. "Promise me you'll do the movie."

None of Ardie's group had any idea why Bill left. Ardie, saddened far more than he would have thought to be, elected to be tactful, and used Bill's disappearance as the occasion to take up with a waiter from Studio who made him ecstatic for three nights and on the fourth stole off with the household cash and a Mucha.

Carla, nostalgically inspired, visited backstage at the first night of an off-Broadway melodrama and took the hero home. It was interesting; but she still hated men.

The Firing Gun told Ardie there would be trouble with Dennis now, perhaps Major Trouble.

"Everyone can be replaced," said Ardie, thumbing through the escort catalogues looking for replicas of Bill Fears.

The Firing Gun made no reply. She had learned, in her long, long life, that not everyone can be replaced. That was what made the social milieu so tense.

"We'll order him a new banana," Ardie went on. "Someone to

take his mind off things. He's so dour when he's thoughtful. Such a moody boy wonder."

"We may have to lose him," said The Firing Gun.

"Oh, please."

"He was useful. So was Bill Fears. But time passes. Voyages end. Great events dissolve. Sweet music grows dark. Sorry. Irritable. We'll find other music."

Ardie sighed. "What is the crop of Hollywood, I wonder?"

"The crop of Hollywood," quoth The Firing Gun, "is new fun." She took the booklet from Ardie, dropped it on a table with the others. "We'll let him go."

Who owned Dennis, then? No one: loneliness is freedom. Once, living in the future, Dennis had sworn off imprudent cabaret. Now he was writing songs no Carla Feller could sing, and when they asked him how he got started in music, he would reply, "I don't know." But that didn't sound right. It began to nag at him: how did he get started in anything? Plodding through his life, saying yes to the movie and letting them harness him into the PR regalia, just being there, just allowing—but keeping his mind clear—he kept running his past through his mind, reviewing his songs. Not till he was riding through the smoky twilight of his sunny L.A. prison town, on his way to a taping, did he at last conceive of the answer to the question.

Mike, about to turn off the television, looked at Erica for the thousandth time that day, but earnestly and quick as a bullet.

They were announcing the guests at the top of a late-night talk show, and Mike had heard Dennis' name.

"Isn't that your brother?" Erica asked.

Dennis, in the studio green room, was sitting between the author of a book advocating child molesting and an actress who had screwed eighty men to get a role in a mini-series. The author looked like a reptile and the actress thought like one.

Do I deserve this? Dennis thought, as his colleagues chatted happily over him.

When he came out on stage, half-smiling in a tie, the audience screamed with delight, though most of them hadn't the vaguest idea who he was.

"He grew a moustache," Erica noted.

Mike cleared his throat. "He's gotten heavier."

"He's a man now, Michael. Just look."

"How did you get started in music?" the host asked.

"When Sneaky Pazillo and my brother Iron Mike smuggled me into the second act of *The Sound of Music.*"

"Christ," said Mike, moving up to the edge of the bed. "That was like twenty years ago."

"Sneaky Pazillo," the host repeated dryly. At his look of detached bemusement, the audience richly giggled.

"Why does he call you Iron Mike?" said Erica. "I've been meaning to ask you that for—"

"*Erica!* How the hell do I get in touch with him?"

One of the girls called out, "Mommy!" and Erica went down the hall.

I wonder if Sneaky is taking this in, Mike thought. I wonder where the neighborhood went to. I wonder what ma would be like now, if she hadn't fallen. Maybe she was a little crazy, but you shouldn't say it like that.

Dennis enlarged on Sneaky's exploits, not omitting the lump of The Cloisters he had secreted in his room.

Erica came in carrying Molleen, Nora trailing drowsily behind. "Daddy," said Molleen sadly, "a giant bit me. Then he flew around."

"Come here, precious." Mike took her from Erica and rocked her in his arms.

"That's your Uncle Dennis, Nora," said Erica, pointing at the television.

"*Really?*"

"He bit Nora, too. And Bobby Jansson. And Miss Carver."

"Miss Carver was in your dream?" Mike asked her.

"Uh-huh. And Mister Rogers' Neighborhood."

"What are you going to sing for us?" the host asked.

"What kind of uncle?" said Nora, watching. "Like Uncle Ron and Aunt Marie?"

"No, those are mommy and daddy's friends. This is your daddy's brother."

"Mister Rogers' Neighborhood bit me, too," said Molleen, tragically.

"It was just a dream, precious."

Molleen eyed the television. "That's the giant who bit me, daddy."

"No, it isn't," said Mike, kissing her nose. "That's my brother Dennis."

At the piano, Dennis sang "Deep-Pocket Party," the number they were using in the movie. Acid voices had ceased to be in by then, but people didn't use their ears: they used their belief in television. A singing video man is worthy by rules of teletronic politics: if you're Among Those Present, you deserve to be.

"There has to be a way," said Mike.

Dennis' television jaunt was the tiniest piece of a PR infiltration that counted manipulations in print and flesh media that cost more than the film itself. The Firing Gun made this her most invigorated project, raising the art of spontaneity to its summit: as when, filming a hot dance sequence in the hearing of reporters with what is called Reach, Carla Feller suddenly broke out of pro, screamed, "Tell him he's not supposed to have hard-ons when he dances with me!", slapped her partner's face, and marched to her dressing room. The next day, half the nation reported the story to the other half.

The climax of all this was the filming of the "Deep-Pocket Party" number: satire on Hollywood to be performed as if it were a salute, and by something like two hundred A-list celebs, singing, dancing, marching, posing, strolling, and—for those who couldn't do any of the above—just standing there. It's the kind of thing that should only be handled on a sound stage; security and commissary considerations alone were beyond what a location setup could guarantee. But The Firing Gun had insisted the number be filmed live in Manhattan on the plaza of a brand-new office tower.

Ardie was amused, but studio chiefs sat dumb, pale, at the very notion. Crazies would be rushing the ropes, actors coking up in public, equipment highjacked. "One of the stars," a producer commented, "might be kidnapped."

"Nevertheless," said The Firing Gun, hoping that one would. "The *aim* is attention," she went on. "The *proof* is attention. *Success* is *attention.*" Conjugate the verb *to schlockerize:* PR is the true auteur.

"Amazing," said Dennis, as he and Carla Feller, both extremely spiffed out, peeped through a window at the hordes of people milling behind the barriers.

"They love us," Carla uttered, though tentatively. She knows they'd love her to death if they got the chance.

"Not them," said Dennis. The construction. "Look. A building is going up in every direction. New York still isn't finished."

Not only were skyscrapers rising, but even quiet little bits were being patched, tucked, perfused. Next to the skeleton of an office tower, a brownstone was being renovated into tiny duplex co-ops. New York is dust and money.

"You know," said Dennis. "I grew up a few blocks from here. It doesn't look that different now, yet the neighborhood is gone. Carla, it's completely gone. Those little places where you'd go for a deluxe, and you had only to walk in for like fifty kids to call out your name. And then it was this big issue about whose table you would sit at, and how popular you were, and who would get sore if you didn't sit with them. You always had your regular place, like the Bon Ton Coffee Shop. And you had your gang, you know, with one guy in it who was your pal, and a few others you sort of liked, or were just used to, and at least one guy you loathed, absolutely loathed."

Outside, the crowd spotted a star and clapped.

"It's funny. I used to think I would have friends like that for the rest of my life. Maybe not those people particularly, but a crowd like that. You know? A gang."

Carla was looking at him. "What's a deluxe?" she asked.

"Hamburger deluxe. French fries and cole slaw. Lettuce. Tomato. Onion. A dumb little pickle impaled on one of those toothpicks wearing a tutu."

"You have a gang, Den."

"It's not the one I wanted. I don't need friends to like me for what I can do. I need friends who liked me before I could do anything. Old friends, who know all my secrets. Neighborhood people. That's what's gone now. People. The neighborhood was people."

Outside, the crowd was getting raucous. Amid the clapping, shocking things were being screamed out, epithets and accusations. Bodyguards lost their formation for a moment, revealing a world-famous hunk, and a woman pressing against the barrier threw a cardboard container of coffee at him, crying, *"You have what I want!"*

"If you like old friends so much," said Carla, "why don't you write about them? 'A Deluxe at the Bon Ton' or something. Doowop. The shuffle. Instead of this stuff about skulls. How that song ever got on the charts . . . I mean, what's a connector?"

William F. MacArt. O'Faiore. Bill Fears.

"And *destroyers*, Den. I mean, we're all in it together, aren't we? What the fuck is a destroyer?"

The Firing Gun, deep in the Hollywood horde with the media facilitators, tuned all else out to hear what Dennis would say. The nine years were up.

"Don't put that song down, Carla. It's the first honest thing I've written. All the others were lies."

"Honeybee, you may write them lies, but when I get through with a song it's honest. Hear?"

"No doubt, lady. But from now on I'm going to be writing songs that you won't be happy to sing."

"Den! How dare you, you traitor?"

"I dare because I have nothing to lose."

186

"They won't let you, Den. They won't."

"I don't believe they can stop me."

The tower melted away as the Witch looked on.

Carla shrugged and Dennis laughed, so Carla laughed too. She loved being in a movie; she loved being in everything she was in. She loved things that act famous. She, too, had what others want. She loved being behind barriers, guarded from the mob. She even loved the danger.

Some of the stars were in hiding, some out socializing with each other. Every so often a guard would fell an intruder from beyond the pale, as food persons passed lunch platters and champagne. Dennis took a helping of tuna-avocado-raisin sandwiches and wandered off to a far corner of the security markout where little could be seen of the movie people and the spectators and guards thinned to almost nothing. A couple of ironworkers were standing there, on lunch break from the job across the street. One of them offered Dennis a puff of toke across the barrier.

Dennis smiled, thinking of Pete Reever, and offered the men a share of his lunch.

"What are those guys like, anyway?" The other ironworker asked him, gesturing at the familiar faces.

"Well, it's relative, isn't it?" said Dennis. "Half of them would only sell you their mothers to get on a magazine cover. The other half would deliver."

Nodding, missing the joke, the hardhats contemplated the greatness spread before them. At their solemn silence, Dennis turned too, relishing the peace of this neglected corner as the known, the promising, the hired, and the rabble surged and shouted.

"You in this show?" one of the men asked Dennis.

Dennis nodded.

"Good luck," said the man.

Dennis looked him in the eye and extended his hand. As they shook, twenty yards beyond, an emerald-green truck bearing a shamrock and the words "Tara Construction Company" began to pull away from the curb at the brownstone site.

"Hey," said Dennis. "That's . . . hey, *look.*"

187

They all looked. What had he seen to make him so still and tight?

"That's it," cried Dennis, starting to move.

He went into business with a building contractor, Bill had said. They renamed the company. It's almost over.

"Hey!" Dennis shouted. *"Wait up!"*

The Firing Gun was out of natural earshot, but she heard all right, and turned, and pushed forward to see Dennis jump the barrier, dodge one guard, and shove his lunch into the face of another. "Hey, *Tara Construction!"* he shouted, heading for the truck, as the sweet music grown sorry perked up, seemed to float on the air in the city's blazing noontime, and then swirled about Dennis as he banged on the side of the truck while trotting beside it, still shouting. At the corner, a red light stopped it and he pulled the door open to confront an angry potbellied man, already climbing out of the cab.

"Don't get mad yet," said Dennis. "Where can I find Michael Keogh?"

"Hey, boss," the man called out as a door slammed on the truck's far side. "Guy here wants Mike Keogh."

"Who wants him?" said Mike, coming into view.

"I do," said Dennis.

Now, it is often told of the old times that there were too many kings in Tara, and too many king's favorites decanting their favors, so that the land was bestrewn with princes and bastards contending their claims on the throne, and killing each other, and dealing with witches for the improvement of their fortunes and the ruin of their rivals'. So was Ireland rent, unable to muster full strength against the Brits. And they tell that, at last, many years after, but two princes were left of all, brothers, and these two fought the final battle for the throne of Tara, each suffering a mortal wound and falling where he stood. And a great wind of wailing rose up and sped through the counties, telling of the passing of the royal house of Tara, and so dreadful was this news that even the Scornful Witch of Fooley made pause in her scheming, and worried, and wept. And that is why there is no king in Ireland now, and no witches.

So they tell. But, as with all legends, this one has its variants. In one, the last two brother princes never met, for the Witch threw a mist about them, and set her banshees to guide it now toward Ballyliffin, now toward Cahersiveen, whithersoever the brothers went, so they could not find each other, nor anything else. And thus they wander still through Ireland, till such time as the Witch deems the land ready to reclaim its notable glory of ancient days.

In another version, the two princes met but did not recognize each other, and passed by without exchanging greetings, and never met again. No one knows what befell them thereafter, though no doubt the Scornful Witch took some roguish part in it.

Yet another account of the tale informs that the two princes agreed to share the kingdom in joint governance, one to reign in the warmth of the year and the other to reign in the cold. And in this version, strange to say, the Witch of Fooley has no role, for —keeping private counsel, giving no reason—she witnessed the meeting of the brother princes, and saw them clasp hands and swear eternal allegiance to each other, and to Tara, and to all their kind. It is not known what the Witch did then, though surely she is somewhere about even today, making her mischief.

"You look great," said Dennis.

Mike went up to Dennis but said nothing.

Horns cursed them as the light changed.

"Boss—"

"Move the truck around the corner," said Mike. "Wait for me." Then he took Dennis' arm and walked him to the sidewalk. "What are you doing here?" he asked in a tone oddly aslant, curious and not curious at once.

Dennis waved at the great Hollywood babble down the street. "I'm in a movie." After a moment, he said, "Iron Mike." A precarious smile.

Mike nodded. "Dennis." A statement of fact.

A pause.

"So you started your own business, after all. I'll bet you're married, too."

"Yeah," said Mike. "Yeah, I'm married. You remember Erica." Speaking slowly, the way men of his class sometimes will when they're winding up for anger. "Got two very pretty little girls. Nora and Molleen."

Dennis fought the impulse to look away by staring at Mike's eyes like a conjurer. "Where do you live?"

"Sea Cliff. Long Island."

"Trees and red wagons," Dennis guessed. "Bicycles in the driveway."

Mike's face flashed a big So what? but he said nothing.

"I've missed you, Iron Mike. I've missed you a lot."

"Yeah, you have? So now you show up after what? Nine years? Loaded, I see. Going Hollywood, right? Show me how prosperous you are. *Huh?* With your Hollywood rhinestone friends. Want to bring them over to pose on my pickup? Take a picture of—" Dennis reached out a hand; Mike slapped it away. "A picture of it! For your Hollywood memory book. Maybe put me in a movie, too, right? *Son of Rocky. Huh?* Maybe we'll do the gay version, call it *Rockette!*" He had grabbed Dennis' hand back and was waving it around. "So you missed me, huh? What about you? You know what it's like trying to get hold of a Hollywood rich kid? Seeing my own brother on television and I can't even say I know him, can I? *Huh?*" He had his arms around Dennis, squeezing him, dizzy with outrage and relief. "You fucking bastard," he said, his voice low. "You goddamn fucking bastard, Dennis."

"I'm sorry, Iron Mike. Jesus, I'm sorry."

Down the street at the edge of the markout, The Firing Gun saw the two of them holding each other, and knew what it was, and made no calculation.

"They've finally locked up the lights," said Ardie, ambling over with a Balkan Sobranie in a diamanté holder. "Where the hell is Dennis?"

The Firing Gun shrugged.

Mike broke the embrace, but held Dennis by the arms. He said, "Don't cry, little brother. I'm sorry, too."

"I can if you can." Dennis wiped Mike's cheek. "Where are you going now?"

"Home."

"Can I come along?"

Why did Dennis apologize to Mike? Was not the older brother's intolerance the cause of their quarrel—his impatience, brutality? Perhaps Dennis is too glad for the reconciliation to worry over niceties of culpability; he wants his family back. Or perhaps he thinks it absurd to measure guilt and innocence at such a solemn moment, and is planning to hit Mike with his thoughts on the matter at some later time. And perhaps Dennis has learned what a very few of us on earth do eventually learn: that to ask forgiveness of those who most wronged us is the profoundest forgiveness of all.

EPILOGUE

The little girls were playing in the front yard when Mike and Dennis drove in. As always, the kids ran up to greet their father, but stepped back as Dennis approached.

"This is your Uncle Dennis," said Mike. "Nora."

"I saw you on television," said the older girl.

"And Molleen."

"If you bite me," Molleen warned, "I'll tell Mommy."

Mike and Dennis took a walk along the road, past friendly houses and uncouth lawns, hosts to the shortcuts of a thousand kids, to talk of Mike's firm and his plans for expansion.

"I have a great idea," said Dennis. "Every businessman wants capital, right? Well, you're the businessman and I've got the capital."

"I don't want your money, sport."

"Someone's got to take it, Iron Mike. It keeps coming in. That's how music works—once you get going, the profits sort of make themselves. I can't afford to bank it. It has to be invested. Okay. Building's on a boom now, and I'd rather invest it with someone I can trust than the usual Hollywood embezzlers. You'd be doing me a favor, believe it or not."

Mike said nothing.

"I know how you feel about rich money. But, you know, I didn't steal it. I earned it. I *wrote* it."

193

"No one's putting you down, little brother."

Dennis stopped walking; Mike turned to him. "Music isn't just a trade, something anyone can enter," said Dennis. "What you are enables you to write. And what I am is . . ." Dennis touched Mike's arm. "What I am is my family. Aunt Molleen, of course, and even Johnny in a strange way. Nora, too. Maybe Nora more than the others." How did you get started in music? "But you're the main one, Iron Mike. So you've got almost as much right to my wealth as I do."

Mike nodded, looked away, exhaled, took a few punches at Dennis' arm, laughed. "Let's get back to the house."

He steered Dennis into the garage. "Something I want you to see here." A rare shy smile. In a back corner, hidden behind cartons and bags of stuff, was Nora's Victrola.

"Jeepers," said Dennis. "Where'd this come from?"

"I thought it was junked with the other stuff when ma died," said Mike, dusting the top with a rag. "Turned out Uncle Flaherty had it. He passed it on to me in his will."

The brothers shared a look. All that building and then death. Uncle Flaherty, now, too. Dennis started to speak, but Mike cut in.

"Some of the records are here," said Mike, hefting a cardboard box. "Tell you what. I'll go inside and you catch up with us in five minutes or so. It's about dinnertime, anyway."

"Iron Mike."

Mike turned back.

"You have a beautiful family."

"Thank you, Dennis." He started off, stopped. "Five minutes, sport—or we'll come get you."

Alone, Dennis pulled up the lid of the Victrola and struck the starting switch. As the turntable slowly began to spin, then picked up speed, Dennis, clutching the sides of the machine, imagined he heard Nora's voice running through her song:

> *One last waltz tonight,*
> *One to conclude the dance,*
> *One last sweetheart's lie takes*

One last hopeless chance.
Sorry lovers swaying,
Sorry music, too.
Tell me you forgive me, dear:
And I'll dance one last waltz with you.

She spoke: "You must never tell him the secret. It was my secret, and the others knew. Now only you know it. Keep it. It would hurt him, and win you nothing."

"I never will tell."

"Swear."

Surprised at the piety come back from the lost and forgot, he knelt and crossed himself.

"Then I'll rest in peace," says she. "Are you well?"

"Yes. Now. I'm going to be an uncle and write wonderful, strange, crazy songs."

"Let me bless you for something. It's easy for us here. Much easier than when you try."

"Isn't mortal prayer effective, then?"

"Almost never. Tell me what you want."

"I want long life and health for Iron Mike and his family."

"I've blessed them for that long since."

"Then I want husbands just like Iron Mike for his daughters when they grow up."

"I'll ask for it. Nothing for yourself?"

"You might put in a word for my health, too. I may need it more than they do, nowadays."

"I'll ask for it. Do you forgive me, little boy?"

"Yes. I believe I do."

She was gone.

Now Dennis opened the box of records. It was right on top— the sorry music of Nora Keogh's bitter cabaret, accidental death by falling. Out with it, play it. One last waltz. Do you want to dance, little boy? As he gave the needle arm a push into the grooves, Dennis looked back on his days, on how he got started: regarded himself at the age of five or so, staring up as he did at the uneasy source of love; and saw his father watching them without seeing, as he would; and Johnny sad because he would never have what he needed; and Mike, who always had it. Something wanted, something known, something done, secrets. Each family bears three, and children tell the history. Families and death. The revenge, the romance, the quest. The connection and destruction, holding people and held people. And Dennis, amazed, thought, Iron Mike is my father.

"Mommy says to take you in to dinner."

Dennis turned with a start. It was Nora. Flesh and blood, his niece.

Molleen joined them. "What's that music?" she asked.

"Listen," said Dennis.

"Can you dance to this?" asked Nora.

"I've danced to worse."

"Show me how."

Dennis took her hands and they moved in great silly circles.

"Can I dance, too?" asked Molleen.

Dennis and Nora took her hands and the three of them waltzed as Mike and Erica stood in the driveway, watching. Mike put his arm around Erica's waist.

"You still haven't told me why he calls you Iron Mike," said Erica.

"Sweetheart," said Mike, "that's a long story."

Dennis stopped moving, but he was smiling, and the two girls danced around him. Families and life. Mike smiled at Dennis.

"Hello, Erica," said Dennis.

The King of Tara had three sons: a warrior, a mason, and a poet. The warrior died in battle. The poet told lies. But the mason made the world.